Jungle Car Pool

Tikiti turned to the window of the passenger side of the cab. An Angolan captain stood on the running board with a Makarov pistol jammed through the open window, pointed at his face. He stared at the Angolan's angry features and slowly raised his hands from the steering wheel.

Suddenly, the Angolan's face exploded. Tikiti screamed with uncontrolled revulsion as the stump of the man's neck pumped twin streams of blood through the window to spatter the front seat.

James Wentworth pushed the headless corpse aside. He didn't even notice the unfired Makarov pistol in the dead man's fist. Wentworth flicked the blood from the blade of his *katana* and returned the samurai sword to its scabbard before he opened the door and climbed in next to Tikiti.

THE HARD CORPS

CORPS

MERCENARY JUSTICE

CHUCK BAINBRIDGE

J

JOVE BOOKS, NEW YORK

MERCENARY JUSTICE

A Jove Book/published by arrangement with
the author

PRINTING HISTORY
Jove edition/January 1988

ISBN: 0-515-09366-1

Jove Books are published by The Berkley Publishing Group,
200 Madison Avenue, New York, New York 10016.
The name "JOVE" and the "J" logo
are trademarks belonging to Jove Publications, Inc.

PRINTED IN THE UNITED STATES OF AMERICA

10 9 8 7 6 5 4 3 2 1

Dedicated to

John Rounds
and
Eliza Shallcross

CHAPTER 1

THE PASSENGERS SHUFFLED into the airport terminal like cattle being herded through a corral. They had just deplaned from a long trans-Atlantic flight and their tired faces and red-rimmed eyes revealed the strain of the trip. Their clothes were wrinkled and stained with sweat.

William O'Neal and James Wentworth III were watching them emerge from gate 23 at John F. Kennedy International Airport. They could see immediately that the passengers came in every shape and size. Many were Americans and Europeans, mostly businessmen and photojournalists. A few were tourists. While many Americans would like to visit Africa, not too many would choose Zaire as the first country they'd visit.

Other passengers were clearly African. Obviously members of the African elite, these men and women appeared well fed, well educated, and very polite. The men wore dark suits with white shirts and skinny striped ties, all of European design. Two women were among the Africans

1

and both were dressed like Jackie Kennedy in the early sixties, complete with long white gloves and cute little pillbox hats.

The male Africans appeared to have suffered little or no jetlag; they smiled and nodded cheerfully at anyone who happened to look in their direction. Their wives were more solemn and avoided looking at the faces that surrounded them.

"That's Jacob." Wentworth nodded as the Africans approached.

O'Neal nodded in turn. He recognized Jacob Zabibu from a recent television interview. The stocky, forty-two-year-old African looked like an ordinary businessman—nothing like the center of a revolution.

Most Americans don't pay much attention to the problems of Africa, aside from the famine in Ethiopia and the racial tensions of South Africa. But O'Neal and Wentworth were very interested. They had a reason to be interested. A professional reason.

O'Neal and Wentworth were the commanding officers of the Hard Corps, an elite team of crack mercenary soldiers. They had formerly served with the Special Forces in Vietnam. Since the war in Southeast Asia, the Hard Corps had gone into business for themselves. Their business was fighting other people's wars. With the arrival of Jacob Zabibu, they knew they'd be seeing action soon.

A week earlier, Zabibu had called a press conference while on a trip to Switzerland to declare the independence of a new central African nation: Kilembe. He was speaking for Ushomba, the acting president. Zabibu stated that Ushomba had the support of the people of this new nation to back his words, and that any attempts to deny his country's independence would be "stopped cold."

This development followed several months of tension in central Africa involving Kilembe and the countries it was seceding from, Zaire and Angola. The world media had looked upon the developments with alarm, seeing Kilembe's independence as another possible African bloodbath, much like Biafra's attempted secession from Nigeria back in the sixties.

Ordinarily, this situation in itself would have invited the active interest of the Hard Corps. War was their business and it looked as if in Kilembe there was going to be a dandy. But in this case, personal reasons for getting involved were also present—reasons important enough for O'Neal and Wentworth to have breached the normal security barriers here at Kennedy, by flashing special cards given them a while back by their contact in the CIA, Joshua St. Laurent. "Damned if these things don't work every time," O'Neal had muttered as the two mercs had entered the customs area of the International Arrivals Building.

Zabibu had arrived, but the Hard Corps didn't want his presence to attract attention. They wanted to meet him before he got out into the crowds. And they'd made sure that this meeting had been kept secret from the media.

Wentworth stepped forward and smiled as Zabibu and his companions drew closer. "*Bonjour*, James," Zabibu announced in his heavy Zaïrois accent. He embraced Wentworth like a long-lost brother. "*Mon vieux.*"

Wentworth smiled, returning the embrace. "*C'est vraiment longtemps,* Jacob," he said.

Wentworth and Zabibu spoke rapidly in French. O'Neal looked on. He had once understood a little French; just enough to help him get laid in the classy sections of Saigon. He had not kept up with the language and could only guess what the two men were talking about. The Hard Corps unit commander ignored the conversation and turned his attention toward Zabibu's companions.

They were young men, well muscled and physically fit. Both wore dark glasses, which gave them a stern, enigmatic look. They stood with their backs straight, feet shoulder-width apart. O'Neal figured Zabibu wasn't traveling with his personal secretary and accountant.

"Jacob," Wentworth said, switching to English. "This is Captain William O'Neal."

"*Enchanté*," Zabibu said, offering his hand to O'Neal. "James has told me a lot about you. I will of course speak English so we may all understand one another."

O'Neal didn't return Zabibu's smile. "Frankly," he said tersely, "I don't want to discuss much of anything in any language until we get out of the airport."

"Of course," Zabibu agreed with a nod. He looked up at O'Neal. The Hard Corps commander was a big guy, about six feet tall with lots of muscles. O'Neal's face was rugged, with deep lines etched in the skin. It was difficult to tell how old O'Neal was. Late thirties or early forties, Zabibu guessed. The mercenary leader's gruff voice sounded as if he had sandpaper in his larynx; his eyes could have been made of steel.

Zabibu knew that O'Neal was a tough son of a bitch who didn't waste time with bullshit. The Hard Corps were supposed to be the best merc team money could buy—and money alone wasn't enough to hire them for a mission. They had to believe in what they were fighting for. If they didn't feel an offer was right, they wouldn't take the job.

The five men walked to the baggage-claim area, where they collected the Africans' luggage. After passing through customs, O'Neal and Wentworth led the Africans through two large doors and out into the swarming crowds awaiting incoming flights. O'Neal smiled: There wasn't a reporter to be seen.

But as the five men hurried through the throngs of people, O'Neal spotted a young bearded man dressed in a dirty old Spanish trench coat. The man's garment was odd, considering it was almost ninety degrees outside. He seemed to be following them, even though he never looked in their direction. In fact, O'Neal thought the kid was trying hard *not* to look at them as he wormed his way through the crowd to remain about fifty feet behind the mercs and the three African visitors.

"I saw him, too," Wentworth whispered to O'Neal.

"Might be a pickpocket or just a weirdo," the Hard Corps boss replied, glad that he wasn't the only one who was paranoid about being followed. "Don't jump to any conclusions."

"What was that?" Zabibu inquired, unable to hear what the two Americans had said.

"We're not sure yet," Wentworth answered. "We'll talk outside, Jacob."

They emerged from the International Arrivals Building. Cabs and limousines flashed by, and people carrying huge amounts of luggage clogged the sidewalk.

Suddenly a green-and-white mini-van appeared among the taxis. It pulled up to the curb. A cabbie honked his horn and shouted an obscenity out a window. The driver of the van replied by thrusting his fist out the window, the middle finger extended and rigid.

"Up yours, shithead!" Joe Fanelli, behind the wheel of the mini-van, barked at the cabbie.

O'Neal, Wentworth, and the three Africans hurried into the van. Fanelli was impatient. "Let's get the fuck outa here," he said, jolting suddenly into the traffic. Several car horns blared protests as the larger vehicle pulled into their path.

"Fuck you!" Fanelli shouted out the window as he steered the van into the right-hand lane. "You'd think all these jerks were on their way to the hospital with wives about to have babies or somethin'. Goddamn New Yorkers are the pushiest cocksuckers in the world."

"You're not making a very good impression on our new clients," Wentworth complained, clearly annoyed by Fanelli's language.

"I'm not making a good impression?" Fanelli gestured at the surrounding traffic. "What about these sons of bitches here? All they know how to use on their cars is the fuckin' horn. They oughtta all get a goddamn broom shoved up their ass.''

"We don't need to hear this, Joe," O'Neal told him as he opened a compartment in the floor of the van.

"This driver is one of your men, Captain?" Zabibu asked, craning his neck to get a better look at Fanelli.

"Sad, but true," Wentworth muttered sourly.

"Fuck you too, Lieutenant," Fanelli growled. "And don't expect me to apologize for sayin' the Big Apple is rotten to the core. I know New York better than any of you guys. Remember, I'm from *Jersey*."

"Can it, Joe," O'Neal ordered. "We might have a problem. Keep an eye open for any cars that might be tailing us.''

"What you mean?" one of Zabibu's bodyguards demanded.

"I think somebody was following us in the airport," O'Neal answered, taking a bundle of thin plastic gloves from the compartment. "Okay. Six pairs. Just enough to go around.''

"What are the gloves for?" Zabibu asked as he watched O'Neal pull on a pair.

"To avoid leaving fingerprints in case things get nasty," the Hard Corps leader replied. He passed the gloves to Wentworth and reached inside the compartment again.

"I don't think this is necessary," Zabibu began. "It is true I have many enemies in Africa, but I doubt that they would be able to reach me here in America—''

"You can't 'doubt it' *too* much or you wouldn't have brought two bodyguards on this trip," O'Neal commented as he extracted a canvas AWOL bag from the floor compartment. "Speaking of which—are you guys heeled?''

"Healed?" A bodyguard frowned, puzzled by O'Neal's question.

"Packing heat," O'Neal explained. "Are you carrying any guns?''

"Guns?" The other bodyguard glared at O'Neal. "*Mais*

non! Airport security is, how you say, much too strict these days. Concern with the hijackings and the terrorism."

"Perhaps we could smuggle guns in airport in Kinshasa," the other protector added, referring to Zaire's capital. "But we thought customs in the United States would be . . . *trop difficile.* Too hard."

"Okay," O'Neal replied. He didn't really give a damn why they didn't have guns. The fact that neither man was armed was all he cared about. "I don't think we've got enough pieces for everybody."

He opened the AWOL bag and started removing plastic bags, which contained .45-caliber 1911A1 Colt semiautomatic pistols. Each bag held one gun and two spare magazines. There were four guns total.

"Joe?" O'Neal began as he handed a pistol to Wentworth. "You packing up front?"

"Sort of," Fanelli replied, watching the road ahead and glancing at the rearview mirror as he drove. "I've got a snub-nose Magnum in a holster hidden under the seat, and an M-26. By the way, I'm wearin' gloves already and I wiped down the vehicle for prints before you guys got on board. Better wipe for prints where you might've touched anything. If you ain't sure, wipe anyway. Can't be too careful."

"Sir," a bodyguard began with a huff. *"S'il vous plaît.* We are not criminals!"

"In the eyes of the law we're committing a number of crimes right now," Wentworth announced as he took a black briefcase from under his seat. "The guns alone violate the 1968 Gun Control Act and New York City's Sullivan Act. We're in an unregistered vehicle with forged license plates. I'd say we're violating enough federal, state, and local laws to wind up in jail for about five to ten years if we get caught."

The bodyguards, whose English was limited, appeared confused. Zabibu quickly translated for them. He looked upset.

"Do you always carry so many weapons and travel in illegal vehicles?" Zabibu asked, staring at Wentworth as if he suddenly doubted that he knew the man.

"Most of the time we carry a lot more firepower than this," Wentworth answered as he tore open a plastic bag and removed a Colt pistol. "We probably violate a lot of laws all the time, but that's just part of the risk that goes with our profession."

Zabibu nodded because he didn't know how else to respond to Wentworth's statement. Indeed, he wasn't sure he knew Wentworth anymore. Perhaps he never had. More than a decade had passed since Zabibu had met Wentworth at an officers' training school at Fort Benjamin Harrison, Indiana.

Wentworth had changed physically, of course. His hair had thinned out and the top of his head was bald. He was a bit thicker around the waist and a little paunchy at the belly. Now Zabibu wondered how much Wentworth's personality had changed over the years.

Lieutenant Wentworth had been an instructor at "Uncle Ben's Rest Home," so called because it consisted of military classrooms rather than concentrating on conventional combat training. Wentworth, Zabibu had learned, was a combat veteran from Vietnam. A highly intelligent officer, Wentworth was a competent instructor, yet less than an inspired teacher. He knew all the information for his classes, could relay it, answer questions, and grade his students; but Wentworth didn't want to be restricted to a classroom. He missed the action and the special camaraderie he'd known with his fellow warriors in Vietnam. Within a year after he'd been transferred to Indiana, Wentworth had resigned his commission and left the United States Army.

Zabibu remembered Wentworth as an intelligent, well-educated man, a Southern gentleman who'd been born and raised in a privileged oil family in Oklahoma. Wentworth had had the blessings of expensive private schools and military academies, including West Point. He was generally polite and formal, frequently carrying a swagger stick and gesturing with it as he spoke.

Wentworth could be a bit arrogant, but he respected strength, something Zabibu with his quiet sense of power practically radiated. Zabibu's English was less than fluent in those days and he was pleased to learn Wentworth spoke excellent French, the official language of Zaire. They discovered common interests and discussed a variety of subjects over a game of chess or afternoon tea.

But a lot can change in ten years. Zabibu had certainly changed. He had been a captain in the Zaïrois paratrooper corps when he had come to America to receive special training in military tactics, piloting the surplus F-14 fighters then being sold to Zaire, and the use of computerized defense weapons employed by modern aircraft.

Now Zabibu was a general commanding the military forces of a new fledgling nation. A desperate nation struggling to be free, in spite of constant pressure from its neighbors, including Zaire. The survival of the Republic of Kilembe might very well depend on whether or not General Zabibu could enlist the special kind of help the men of the Hard Corps could provide.

"Hey, Captain," Fanelli announced. "We're approaching the Triboro Bridge. We'll be in Manhattan in a few minutes."

"Nobody following us yet?" O'Neal asked as he stuck a .45 Colt into his waistband and put the spare mags in his jacket pockets.

"Nope," Fanelli answered, slowing the van as they reached the bridge. "But that doesn't mean we're in the clear. Trying to tail another vehicle in this kind of traffic would be almost impossible unless you could get right on the other guy's ass the second he left the airport and stayed on him all the way. If somebody hired some local talent to deal with us, they'll know better than to try that."

"What do you think they might do?" O'Neal asked, glancing out the window at the crush of traffic. Cars zipped in front of one another and cut each other off so often O'Neal was astonished no one crashed. He figured Fanelli had a point.

"If they know Zabibu has reservations at a hotel in Manhattan, I'd guess they have people waiting for us at the other side of the bridge," Fanelli said. "Guy you spotted at the airport was probably just a scout to alert the real hit team and let 'em know what kinda vehicle to look for and to tell 'em how many people they'll have to take care of."

"Isn't it possible the man you saw at the airport wasn't following us, Captain O'Neal?" Zabibu asked as he looked at his bodyguards. They were checking the pistols O'Neal had given them before concealing them under their jackets.

"Sure," O'Neal agreed. "And if we're lucky that's the way things'll turn out. We still have to be ready for trouble just in case. In our profession, you never assume you're safe."

"I think you jump at shadows," a bodyguard complained. "If the enemy was here in New York and they knew about the general—what flight he on, what hotel he at—then surely they would assassinate him at the hotel, not on the streets."

"That might depend on how they want to kill him," O'Neal stated. "Could be they don't want a political assassination that'll look like a political assassination."

"I think Bill has a point," Wentworth commented. "After all, Jacob, if you get killed by a sniper bullet in your hotel room or you pick up the phone to call room service and the receiver explodes with enough C-4 plastic explosives to blow your head off, it will be quite obvious you were murdered for political reasons. However, an 'accident' or a freak incident that might be considered a 'street crime' might allow your assassins to avoid direct blame."

"That would be a great deal of trouble to go to just to kill me," Zabibu said with a smile. "The notion is almost flattering."

"Well, it's not the president of your fan club who'd be out to have you killed," O'Neal told him. "So try not to be too flattered."

The van crossed the Triboro Bridge. The passengers had a good view down the East River—which looks a lot better from a distance than up close. Tugboats churned across the murky waters and sea gulls hovered above the rippling surface. Ahead of the van lay the skyscrapers of Manhattan. Fanelli commented that Manhattan's reputation as the "jewel of the Hudson" was part of an advertising conspiracy by Madison Avenue promoters. Not surprising, he claimed, because Madison Avenue is part of Manhattan.

"Of course, the *real* jewel is on the opposite side of the Hudson River," Fanelli continued as he drove the van downtown. "Good old Jersey."

"Oh, God," Wentworth groaned. "After years of hearing you tell horror stories of growing up in the slums of Jersey City, now you're claiming it's the center of Western civilization."

"Compared to New York," Fanelli insisted. "I tell ya, everything that's wrong with Jersey could be solved if we blew up the Holland Tunnel—"

Suddenly a Chevy station wagon bolted from the curb at the corner of Lexington Avenue and Eighty-sixth Street. It bullied past traffic waiting for the light to change. The station wagon scraped the side of a checker cab and shoved a Ford Tempo into the next lane. A man on a Yamaha motorcycle screamed as the wagon rammed his bike. Rider and machine hurtled into the intersection, straight into the path of an oncoming garbage truck. The Yamaha crunched against the frame of the heavy truck while the unlucky motorcyclist tumbled under the front tires of the garbage-collection rig before the horrified driver could stomp on the brake.

"Shit!" Fanelli exclaimed as he tried to weave clear of the garbage truck.

The van clipped the tail end of the truck. A Honda smashed

into the flank of Fanelli's vehicle, but without apparent serious damage.

The station wagon skidded to a stop in front of the van. Car doors popped open and three men dressed in baggy old clothes and stocking masks jumped from the wagon. Each held a pump shotgun with a cut-down barrel. One man raised his weapon to point the big black muzzle at the windshield of the van while the other two tried to attack the vehicle from both sides.

"Down!" Fanelli shouted as he ducked low and tromped the gas pedal.

The van shot forward. A burst of shotgun pellets smashed into the windshield and punched a network of spiderweb patterns in the thick glass. Shards of glass fell into Fanelli's hair as the ballsy kid from Jersey held on to the steering wheel and kept moving.

Another shotgun roared and buckshot shattered a side window at the back of the van. O'Neal, Wentworth, Zabibu, and one of the bodyguards stayed low, but the other protector chose the wrong moment to raise his head. Several Number 4 buckshot pellets splintered the African's frontal bone and tore into his brain. The man fell dead on the floor of the van.

Fanelli stayed low and kept the van on a rocketing collision course with the station wagon. A shotgun-toting hood tried to pump the action of his weapon to eject a spent shell casing from the 12-gauge blaster and feed another round into the chamber. The nose of the van crashed into the gunman and rammed the Chevy wagon.

The hoodlum's torso was crushed like a tomato in a steel vise. Caught between the unstoppable van and the immovable station wagon, his ribs and spine crunched apart. His mangled corpse convulsed feebly and slumped against the steel frame of the wagon.

Another shotgunner worked the pump to his Winchester riot piece and fired a burst of buckshot through the side windows of the van. Glass showered the backs of the passengers in the back of the rig. O'Neal low-crawled to the rear of the vehicle, wiggling on his belly while using his elbows to propel his body across the narrow floor.

"Stay down!" Wentworth yelled to Zabibu and the surviving bodyguard as he drew his .45 Colt from his belt and thumbed off the safety.

"Don't worry," the general assured him, crawling to the corpse of the other bodyguard to pry the unused Colt pistol from the dead man's hand.

Wentworth moved to the windows that had been blown away by the last shotgun blast. He saw O'Neal was already in position at the rear of the van. The Hard Corps commander nodded at Wentworth to let the lieutenant know he was ready.

Fanelli reached overhead from his awkward position low in the front seat and grabbed the gearshift. He put the van in reverse and shoved on the gas. The van rolled backward as a shotgun blast pelted the front of the rig. A side window shattered and more glass shampooed Fanelli's hair. None of the buckshot scored a direct hit on the door and no pellets pierced the thick metal skin.

Another shotgun volley tore into the right rear tire, shredding rubber and mangling the hub. O'Neal raised his .45 and pointed it at a side window at the rear of the vehicle. The merc boss kept his head down and fired through the glass pane. O'Neal didn't intend to shoot any of the gunmen; he just wanted to get the attention of the buckshot-throwing bastard on that side of the van.

Wentworth carefully raised his head and peered out a window. He saw O'Neal's distraction had worked. The gunman outside the van was pointing his Winchester pump at the rear of the vehicle. Wentworth immediately thrust his Colt pistol through the jagged gap in the window and aimed at the hoodlum's upper body.

The lieutenant squeezed the trigger. A 185-grain hollowpoint projectile smashed into the collarbone of the shotgun-

ner. The man screamed as the force of the big bullet spun
him around. The guy managed to hold on to his Winchester
with his left hand, although his right arm hung useless from
a shattered joint.

Wentworth fired another .45 round through the center of
the gunman's chest. The man's feet whipped up from the
street and his body fell hard. The shotgun clattered uselessly
to the ground beside his trembling form. His body soon
ceased to move as the final muscle reflex performed its last
twitch.

The driver of the station wagon staggered from the car,
a .38 Smith & Wesson revolver in his fist. He ducked behind
the Chevy for cover and aimed the gun across the hood of
the car. The remaining shotgunner realized the men inside the
van were armed. He fired another burst of buckshot at the
vehicle as he ran backward toward the station wagon. Pellets
slammed into the front of the van, tearing metal and punctur-
ing a front tire.

Fanelli suddenly sat up in the front seat. He saw the
hoodlum work the pump to his shotgun and quickly poked
the two-and-a-half-inch barrel of a stainless-steel Ruger Se-
curity-Six through the largest gap in the broken windshield.
Fanelli triggered the snub-nose revolver twice. Two .357
slugs ripped into the chest of the enemy gunman before the
son of a bitch could aim his Winchester.

The high-velocity bullets punched through the man as if
he were made of Styrofoam. The Magnum rounds obliterated
the thug's heart before his body hit the pavement. Fanelli
instinctively ducked after delivering his .357 messengers.
Just in time, because the hood at the wagon pumped two
bullets into the windshield a split second later.

Sirens wailed as two police cars tried to cut through traffic
without slamming into frightened pedestrians who ran in all
directions to avoid getting involved in the gun battle. Several
cops advanced on foot, carrying service revolvers and riot
guns.

"Drop the gun!" a policeman shouted as he aimed his piece at the hoodlum stationed by the Chevy.

The thug whirled and fired his .38 in the general direction of the cop's voice. One bullet hit the officer under the ribs, but he triggered his service revolver before he went down. Three other cops also opened fire, including one officer with a 12-gauge. Bullets and buckshot smashed the gunman's body into bloodied pulp. His corpse was barely recognizable as human by the time it slumped to the pavement.

"Shit," Fanelli muttered, peering out the van at the blue-uniformed figures that had arrived at the scene. "The cops are here. What do we do now?"

"Will the van still run?" O'Neal asked as he moved toward the front of the vehicle.

"You kiddin'?" Fanelli replied, rolling his eyes toward the ceiling of the van. "This heap will be lucky if it can get sold for scrap."

O'Neal scanned the streets, looking for an avenue of escape. The pedestrians had all run for cover. Most New Yorkers have developed special urban survival instincts and only a moron would stand out in the open when bullets and buckshot were heating up the air. The cops were still out there, of course. O'Neal saw two officers kneeling beside the policeman who'd caught a bullet. At least three more had weapons pointed at the van.

A number of stores were near their position, but fleeing into one of these would only be running from one boxed-in coffin to another. Odds were they wouldn't reach cover anyway. O'Neal realized there were probably more cops out there than what he could see from his limited viewpoint. More cops were certainly on their way to back up the police already at the scene.

Then O'Neal spotted the subway entrance, less than twenty yards away. Not far to run, but far enough for the police to cut them down before they could reach the stairs.

The Hard Corps leader was about to suggest that Zabibu

and his bodyguard step forward with their hands raised and surrender to the police. After the cops learned who Zabibu was they wouldn't keep him long. A good bullshit story would convince the police and the mayor's office that the Africans had been victims of circumstance who'd gotten tangled up with a gun battle between warring criminal gangs. They'd believe it because they'd *want* to believe it.

While Zabibu stepped into view for the cops, the three Hard Corps mercs would make their move. With a little luck—actually a lot of luck—they might be able to reach the subway while the police were distracted. Not a very great plan, O'Neal realized, but it seemed to be the only choice they had. The Hard Corps couldn't afford to stand trial and they damn sure didn't intend to shoot it out with the NYPD. Hell, the mercenaries and the cops were really fighting for the same causes, even if their methods differed. Shooting a police officer would be like killing one of themselves.

Suddenly three more goons in stocking masks appeared from an alley. One guy carried an Ingram MAC-10 machine pistol while the other two held lever-action Marlin rifles.

The Ingram sprayed a murderous salvo of 9 mm parabellum rounds at three surprised cops. One officer fell, his short-sleeve shirt ripped up with bullet holes. Another screamed and stumbled into a doorway, two bullets in his right leg. The third managed to duck behind a car without receiving any parabellum manglers.

"The subway!" O'Neal pointed as a .30-30 rifle slug burrowed into a door of the van.

"But—" Zabibu began. Wentworth grabbed his arm and hauled him to a door.

"There isn't time to argue!" the lieutenant declared.

O'Neal emerged from the vehicle first and moved to the front of the van, using the rig for cover. He tried to locate the enemy and the police officers among the surrounding vehicles and buildings. Cars, cabs, and buses had been abandoned by drivers and passengers when possible. Others had chosen to lie low and pray they'd survive the ordeal. Fortunately, none of the civilians were moving around much. Just cops and bad guys.

Only one gunman was firing his Marlin .30-30 at the van. The other two were busy holding the police at bay. The guy with the Ingram was using a parked sedan for cover with a rifleman to cover his back. The other Marlin sniper remained at the mouth of the alley while trying to pump .30-30 rounds into the van.

The cops seemed to have their hands full with the enemy gunmen for the moment. O'Neal gestured for the others to run for the subway. They bolted for the subterranean sanctuary while O'Neal stayed by the van to cover their backs.

The sniper was the first to see the four figures dart for the subway. He aimed his rifle at their backs. O'Neal realized the rifleman was beyond effective handgun range. He elevated his pistol, aimed, and fired high to compensate for the extra distance. Gravity brought the projectile down in an arch and the slug sparked against brick near the mouth of the alley. The sniper recoiled with surprise and alarm.

However, a cop misunderstood O'Neal's actions and fired two .38 rounds at the Hard Corps commander's position. Bullets ricocheted against the frame of the van and O'Neal was forced to stay down. This allowed the alley sniper enough time to aim his Marlin and fire at Wentworth, Zabibu, Fanelli, and the bodyguard.

A .30-30 slug tore into the nape of the bodyguard's neck. The African fell forward and landed face-first on the sidewalk. Wentworth glanced down at the body and immediately realized the man was dead, spinal cord severed, vertebrae shattered. He urged the others to keep going.

The Ingram erupted, blasting a trio of parabellums across the chest of the policeman who'd tried to take out O'Neal. The cop tumbled to the pavement in a twitching heap, but his assassin had raised head and shoulders above the hood of the sedan only thirty feet from O'Neal's position.

The Hard Corps OIC was an excellent pistol marksman and he'd hit smaller targets before at a greater range. O'Neal hastily aimed the Colt with both hands and fired. A .45-caliber slug smashed into the Ingram gunner's face, just below the left eye. The bullet split cheekbone and cracked the eye socket. A chunk of the man's face became a crimson smear and the back of his head blossomed in a hideous spray of brains and skull fragments.

The sniper triggered his Marlin and a rifle round burst the headlight next to O'Neal's left forearm. The merc captain cursed and drew back from the line of fire, but he glimpsed a policewoman bob up from behind a taxicab. She was pretty cute for a cop, with curly brown hair and breasts that practically spilled out of her uniform shirt. She was holding her service revolver in a proper Weaver's combat grip as she squeezed the trigger twice.

The policewoman fired both rounds into the alley. One .38 Special slug hit the sniper in the sternum and the other tore into the hollow of his throat. The guy dropped his Marlin and clutched at his throat as he stumbled out of view, mortally wounded.

O'Neal saw the barrel of the remaining gunman's rifle appear from the rear of the sedan. The bastard seemed to be aiming his Marlin at the lady cop. O'Neal figured he owed her a favor and quickly fired a .45 round into the window to the left rear door of the sedan. The bullet blew a hole in the glass and passed through the interior of the car to smash the window to the right door as well.

The rifle barrel disappeared from view. O'Neal wasn't sure if he'd hit the bastard, but the trick convinced him to lie low, and that was good enough. The lone rifleman wouldn't last very long against the police. If the cops didn't kill him, the guy would probably surrender when he ran out of ammo.

O'Neal figured he'd done enough to help the boys and girls in blue. He thrust the warm barrel of the Colt .45 into his belt and dashed for the subway. The sixth sense of a combat veteran signaled danger as he ran for the stairs to the subway. Yet he reached the entrance without receiving a bullet between the shoulder blades.

Maybe I just imagined it, O'Neal thought as he jogged down the stone steps to a dark tunnel below. *After all, nobody's perfect.* There was no reason to believe one's survival senses might not get a message wrong under stress — assuming one even believes such a sixth sense exists. *Or maybe,* O'Neal thought, *just maybe one of the cops had a gun aimed at my back and then held his fire. Maybe it was even the lady cop.*

That notion appealed to him.

CHAPTER 2

"NOW, DIDN'T I tell you what to expect from New Yorkers?" Fanelli remarked as he held on to a hand strap on the downtown IRT.

"I wish you'd shut up, Sergeant," Wentworth muttered. The lieutenant sat in an aisle seat next to the standing Fanelli, pretending to read a newspaper he'd picked up from the floor.

O'Neal and Zabibu sat next to each other toward one end of the car. The Hard Corps commander didn't like traveling on the subway. The train was crowded and noisy. It smelled of sweat and stale urine. Or maybe the odor came from the dirty old raincoat O'Neal wore. He'd gotten the piece of trash from a homeless man on the subway platform. O'Neal had given the bum his sports jacket and ten dollars for the coat.

O'Neal had made this outrageous trade in order to change his appearance from what the police APB would have as his description. The derelict sure had good reason to be happy. Wentworth had also paid the guy ten bucks for a dirty old porkpie hat and then given him another ten just to leave the station and forget he'd ever met them. The bum had eagerly agreed to the first and, Wentworth knew, as soon as he reached a bar or liquor store he'd start working on the latter.

Fanelli and Zabibu had also made a few changes. Since the general's black business jacket, necktie, and horn-rimmed glasses would certainly be mentioned in any description by the police, Zabibu had somehow removed all four while standing in between subway cars. He'd thrown the clothes off the train and pocketed the glasses. Fanelli removed his red windbreaker and disposed of it in the same manner. His T-shirt was olive-drab green with two crossed M-16 rifles and the legend ''Let's Party'' on the front. Since the shirt wouldn't have been noticed by the cops, it was safe to keep it.

A newsstand back at the station had supplied them with other items for emergency disguise. They had purchased a cheap pair of plastic sunglasses for Fanelli and a pair of wire-rim models for Zabibu. An ''I Love NY'' baseball cap was bought for the general as well as a flimsy sweatshirt with the same motto.

Wentworth also disposed of his suit jacket and exchanged his houndstooth necktie for a clip-on bowtie from the brief-case he'd taken from the van. He had removed the contents from the valise before kicking it under a bench at the station. Among the items from the case were a pair of reading glasses, which the merc lieutenant donned, and a folding umbrella, which he tucked under his arm, even though it was cloudless outside.

''You look like a walking advertisement for Nerds Unlimited,'' Fanelli commented when he saw the alterations Wentworth had made.

''That's rather the idea,'' the Hard Corps XO replied,

pretending he didn't find the disguise embarrassing.

They also now had a large "I Love NY" shopping bag to hide the guns in. O'Neal had covered these up with a handful of porno magazines he'd bought at the newsstand. But the most vital part of their disguise was to separate so it appeared they were not traveling as a group. Only O'Neal and Zabibu seemed to be together. Fanelli had suggested they take the train as far as it would go in Brooklyn, then get off and take a cab back into Manhattan.

"Okay, General," O'Neal began as he sat with Zabibu at one end of the car. He felt the loudness of the subway would mask their conversation. "Suppose you tell me what the hell's going on?"

"If you want to know who's trying to kill me," the general began, "I can't really give you a name, but no doubt opponents of the Republic of Kilembe are responsible."

"I gathered that," O'Neal remarked sourly. "Don't tell me, I can guess. The hit was probably ordered by the government of one of the countries that are pissed off because Kilembe has declared independence as a separate nation. That list includes at least two African countries that believe Kilembe is their territory."

"I see you've taken an interest in my homeland," Zabibu remarked, nodding slightly. "What do you know about us?"

"Just what I've read and heard on the news," the mercenary answered. "You and Acting President—Ushomba, right?—have declared that some land in parts of Zaire and Angola is now an independent nation."

"It is a new nation and no longer part of either of the countries you mentioned," Zabibu insisted. "It is my homeland."

"The governments of Zaire and Angola don't agree," O'Neal stated.

"Of course they don't," Zabibu said. "Which is why we must defend our freedom."

O'Neal continued. "Those governments think you're traitors to your 'real' country."

"Traitors?" Zabibu raised his eyebrows. The train halted briefly at a station, and Zabibu waited for the doors to close before continuing. "Were the founders of the American Revolution traitors because they wanted independence from British rule?"

"I didn't say I agreed with their opinion," O'Neal assured him. "But you must admit that's how they look at you."

Zabibu sighed. "I know, Captain, I know. Far better than you could ever know. Do you know what we're trying to do in Kilembe, Captain?" Zabibu pulled off his dark glasses to look at O'Neal's face more clearly. "We're trying to establish a real democratic republic with a constitution that will protect the rights and freedoms of its citizens. An African nation founded on the same great principles as that of the United States of America." Two kids with a blaring ghetto blaster maneuvered their way through the crowded subway car. "Do you have any idea how fortunate you are to have been born in this country?"

"Yeah," O'Neal replied. "I've seen how people live in a lot of other countries. I've seen how their governments operate and how little freedom exists in 'em. Freedom means a lot to me, General. That's why I'm a mercenary."

"Indeed?" Zabibu seemed intrigued. "I don't see the connection."

"A regular soldier fights wars because his government chooses to get involved in the conflicts," O'Neal explained. "That's called patriotism, right? Unless we're talking about the guy on the other side. If he's fighting for another government then he's a brainwashed fanatic. A mercenary doesn't fight because a government orders him to do it. He fights because it's his choice."

"Some would say you fight for money," Zabibu commented.

"No mercenary is in the business just for the money,"

O'Neal told him. He eyed suspiciously a scuzzy-looking man sitting across from them. But the man got off at the next stop. "A merc can make a lot of money—if he lives long enough. But there are other ways to make a lot of money without risking your life every time you're out of town on business. Mercenaries do their job because they enjoy it and they believe in what they're doing."

"We believe in what we're doing, too," the African declared. "Are you aware that no African country has a truly democratic government? None can honestly claim to be a republic with a constitution and a genuine representative government fairly elected into office by the people."

"That's what I've heard," O'Neal said with a shrug. "To be honest, we've never had a mission in Africa. We had hoped to join a group of freedom fighters in Uganda back in the seventies. They were trying to overthrow Idi Amin. Turned out they were a Marxist outfit being backed by Cubans from Angola. So we didn't go. Uganda might have been better off under Communist rule than to be ruled by a butcher like Amin, but another Marxist country in Africa sure wouldn't be in the best interests of the United States."

"It's much the same everywhere," Zabibu sighed. "So-called freedom fighters fighting for one tribe, one ideology. So little true freedom anywhere in Africa. Zaire itself, which claims me as its citizen, is a one-party dictatorship. Zaire isn't in the Soviet camp, but the government is almost as repressive as those of Angola and other nearby countries, like the Congo. The state confiscated the rights to businesses and plantations in Zaire. The central government controls and owns all businesses, trade, industries, and distribution of goods and services. That's not freedom, Captain O'Neal."

"And you think Kilembe will change that?" The merc frowned.

"Of course, we realize that Zaire and Angola will try to

destroy us. It is inevitable that they try," Zabibu said as
the subway stopped briefly at a station.

"You remember what happened to Biafra?" O'Neal
asked.

"I remember," Zabibu replied with a solemn nod.
"Biafra declared its independence of Nigeria in 1967. They
suffered three years of war and starvation before the Biafran
republic collapsed. However, we have a different situation
in Kilembe."

"Sure you do," O'Neal snorted. "Instead of pissing off
one big country that wants to whip your ass, you've pissed
off *two* of 'em. One of those countries has the Soviet Union
for a Dutch uncle and is crawling with Russian and Cuban
troops. I fail to see any advantage."

"You would if you understood the nature of politics in
Africa, my friend." Zabibu smiled as the subway jolted to
a start again. "Zaire is reluctant to take direct military action
against our nation because part of our republic is situated
on territory Angola claims as its own. If Zaire invades us,
they may be accused of attacking Angola. This could lead
to war between those countries. Zaire doesn't want to risk
that."

"Angola feels the same way about risking a war with
Zaire?" O'Neal asked.

"Captain," Zabibu said, "the tiny Republic of Kilembe
isn't worth a major war. Neither of the countries involved
in this dispute wants to risk that possibility."

"So they're not going to take military action," O'Neal
said. "But if that's true, I don't see why you're talking
about having to defend yourself, or why you want to hire
a bunch of mercenaries."

"When I speak of defense, I do not mean against a military
invasion," Zabibu explained. "Right now that is not our
worry. Terrorist strikes have been occurring in Kilembe.
Well-armed attacks on civilians. Our people aren't prepared
to deal with this sort of guerrilla warfare. Most Kilembans

are farmers, plantation workers, or miners. Our armed forces are too small and inexperienced to deal with this problem.''

The subway arrived at a major stop and most people got off, only to be replaced by another crowd of people.

O'Neal looked thoughtfully down at a skin magazine atop the shopping bag between his feet. "I see," he said after a pause. "So you want to hire the Hard Corps to train your military in antiterrorist tactics and counterwarfare against jungle guerrillas.''

"That's exactly what we have in mind!" Zabibu smiled. "Naturally, you'll want us to participate in some of the actions against the enemy as well.''

"Of course.''

"Well," O'Neal began, "that presents some problems. Working as a mercenary is always borderline as far as the legality of the profession is concerned. Some missions are more legal than others, but what you're suggesting will require my team to virtually join your military. We'd actually be commanding soldiers in the armed forces of a foreign government.''

Zabibu was briefly distracted by a fat woman trying to squeeze by him. "Is that a problem?" he asked.

"It could be if the United States government finds out about it," O'Neal replied. "Serving in another nation's armed forces could be regarded as an act of treason, even if these actions don't jeopardize the interests of the United States. For this resaon, I must insist that we be officially 'attached' to your military as 'independent instructors and observers.' Agreed?"

"Of course," Zabibu assured him.

"Another problem is time," O'Neal continued, reaching for a pack of cigarettes in his shirt pocket, which had somehow come through the gun battle. He glanced up at a graffitti-covered NO SMOKING sign and left his cigarettes where they were. "Frankly, we've got a lot of expenses to take care of and we're always looking for assignments that pay big money. The Hard Corps has been paid as much as two million dollars for a mission. Considering the condition of your country, I doubt if you have much in the way of liquid assets at this time.''

"We can't afford to pay you two million dollars,'' Zabibu admitted as the train slowed to a stop in between stations. "At least, not all at once. Actually, I am authorized to pay your group only two hundred thousand dollars in Swiss bank notes.''

O'Neal lowered his voice; the train had stopped. ''I'm not gonna waste time haggling about the fee, General,'' O'Neal told him. ''Let's cut through the bullshit. Two hundred thousand is your original offer, right? If I refuse you take it higher and then I'm supposed to come down a little and eventually we agree on a fee. Skip that crap and give me the bottom line. How much?''

The subway jolted to a start again and crawled forward. ''A hundred thousand in advance,'' Zabibu stated. ''Another hundred thousand after you arrive in Kilembe and begin work. In the future we will pay you an additional three hundred thousand dollars after our economy is stabilized and Kilembe can afford the payments.''

''We don't generally work that way.'' O'Neal frowned. ''Figure on a hundred grand up front to cover our travel expenses and other costs. After we complete our mission we'll want an additional two hundred thou. If one or more of us gets killed, the survivors get the full amount. I want that in writing. We've got a lawyer who'll draw up the contract.''

''You're serious?'' the general said with a smile.

''Damn right,'' O'Neal said with a nod. ''Our attorney has connections with law firms in other countries and they'll be able to sue your government if we don't get paid. I don't know where you'd find yourself in court, but you'd better believe it would happen. A few clients in the past have tried to rip us off, but nobody has ever gotten away with it. Just a precaution.''

"I'll have to make a phone call before I can agree to that," Zabibu replied.

"Sure," O'Neal agreed. "I have to check with my partners to be sure the terms are agreeable to them as well. Finally, we have to agree to a time limit for our mission. Training your troops and participating in counterterrorist actions without even putting a dent in the enemy's activities could go on for years. The other side has a lot more manpower. We can't afford to set up shop in Kilembe indefinitely. So, let's say we'll agree to four months in your country. If we have to stay there any longer than that it'll cost you."

"I thought you believed in what we're doing, Captain," Zabibu sighed, disappointed.

"I do," O'Neal assured him. "I also believe in money. The Hard Corps is gonna make a profit on this mission, General. Win or lose. To be honest, I think your republic is a very noble experiment, but Biafra was a noble experiment, too. Katanga—remember that, in Zaire?—was a noble experiment. If your country even exists for four more months it'll be a miracle."

"If you believe that," Zabibu began, "why would you even consider this mission?"

"Because you're an old friend of Jim Wentworth," the Hard Corps commander answered. "He speaks quite highly of you and Jim doesn't usually say much good about anybody except Robert E. Lee and Toshiro Mifune. I figure you must be special and whatever you're doing in Kilembe must be pretty goddamn good. Besides, from time to time we can be a little idealistic ourselves."

"That can be dangerous," Zabibu said with a smile.

CHAPTER 3

STEVE CAINE HEARD the gunshots. He recognized the sound as the report from a large-caliber rifle. The shots were at least four seconds apart. Bolt-action rifle, he thought. Probably a hunter somewhere near the compound.

Caine spent much of his time in the forest within the five hundred acres of the compound. The area was ideally suited for the needs of the Hard Corps. Located in a remote section of the state of Washington, the compound had formerly been the property of a band of marijuana ranchers who'd gotten rugged by the DEA. The pot plantation owners needed lots of money to pay for lawyers and they eagerly sold the land to the Hard Corps for a ridiculously low price per acre.

The marijuana had been dug up and carted away by the DEA for evidence. That was fine with the Hard Corps. They needed a base of operations, not a lifetime supply of weed. The natural resources of the region offered them exactly what they wanted. The forest provided the mercs with desirable camouflage of spruce, fir, and Western hemlock trees. Streams and freshwater lakes offered clean drinking water and a variety of fish. Mule deer and an occasional elk entered the area. Other animals also passed through from time to time, including bears, raccoons, bobcats, and coyotes. Caine had even found the pawprint of a mountain lion among the tracks of their animal visitors.

A dam provided power with hydroelectric generators. But the Hard Corps didn't limit themselves to a single source of energy. They also built windmill-powered generators and solar-operated battery units. The mercs kept a number of diesel generators for backup if all else failed.

The Hard Corps had a motor pool with trucks, jeeps, and motorcycles. A small airstrip handled two helicopters—a Bell UH-1D troop transport and a Huey Cobra gunship. The Cobra remained at the copterpad. The other three members of the Hard Corps had left in the Bell chopper five days ago. They'd gone to Seattle to make arrangements for their trip to New York to meet Zabibu. They didn't need Caine in New York and he didn't want to join them.

The tall bearded mercenary had formerly been a product of towns and cities. Caine had been born to a middle-class family at the outskirts of Detroit. Yet he had never truly considered himself to be a city person.

He had always been a loner and a social misfit. Caine never seemed to fit in anywhere as a youth. He didn't even seem to belong with his own family, and when he married and tried to raise a new family, the effort failed miserably. Within a year after high school, Caine was divorced and wandering about like a broken, dazed zombie.

An encounter with some violent hoboes led to his arrest and trial. The judge gave him a choice: he could go to jail or enlist in the military. Caine chose the latter and joined the United States Army. Remarkably, the bitter loner discovered physical and mental abilities he had never realized he possessed. He even decided to opt for Special Forces to put himself to the supreme test of training and conditioning.

Of course, the real test had been in Vietnam. The hardships and carnage of the battlefields were a terrible experience, but Caine hadn't expected war to be pleasant. He discovered that soldiers in combat care for one another with greater feeling than most brothers. This common bond was a new experience for Caine. He had finally found a family.

This family was the Special Forces team that came to be known as the Hard Corps. The three guys who meant the most to him were Captain O'Neal, Lieutenant Wentworth, and Sergeant Fanelli. More than a dozen of their fellow Green Berets were killed or seriously wounded during their missions in 'Nam, yet the four battle-hardened pros seemed almost invincible. They eventually became a legend within the ranks of American servicemen in Southeast Asia.

Caine also fell in love with a Katu woman named Tran Mai. The Katu were Montagnards, primitive tribesmen who occupied the central and northern highlands of Vietnam. The " 'Yards" had learned to distrust and despise the Vietnamese—North or South. Yet, no one was better suited to assist troops in the mountain regions than the Montagnards, and the American Special Forces were eager to enlist the 'Yards as allies.

The Katu had a reputation as the fiercest and most warlike of all the Montagnards. Even the other mountain tribes feared the Katu. Few dared to attempt contact with the Katu, but Steve Caine accepted the risks and learned all he could about their culture, customs, and language.

The risks were very real. The Katu were excellent hunters and trackers. They were also experts in stealth, camouflage, and night fighting. The Katu's skill in silent death was almost supernatural. Their laws could often be quite ruthless. Executions and even human sacrifice were among their customs.

Caine got to know the Katu as few outsiders ever did.

He gained their trust and respect and enlisted their aid for several Special Forces operations. He also married Tran Mai. This marriage ended more tragically for Caine than the first: Tran Mai was killed by an NVA assault force in 1972.

The Americans pulled out of Southeast Asia, but Steve Caine remained. His war was not over. Caine slipped away from his unit and joined the Katu. He became a warrior within the tribe and learned to handle the war lance and bow and arrows with deadly skill. He became an expert in booby traps and concealment. Caine learned to move as silently as a shadow and as cunningly as a snake.

However, primitive weapons were no match for superior numbers and modern firepower. Inevitably, the Katu suffered losses. One by one, Caine's Katu brothers died. In the end, only Steve Caine remained. In 1975, he finally decided it was time to leave Vietnam. He trekked across Laos, then slipped into Thailand with no idea of what to do next.

Ironically, he learned of a team of mercenaries who were allegedly in Thailand to launch a rescue mission into Laos to liberate American POWs supposedly being held at a prison camp near Phu Bia. Caine decided to meet with the mercs and ask to join them. To his astonishment, he discovered O'Neal, Wentworth, and Fanelli were the leaders of the outfit. And so the Hard Corps was reunited once more.

Caine had returned to the States with his three Hard Corps partners, but part of him never left Vietnam. Walls and roofs seemed like prison cells to Caine. He spent as much time as possible living off the land as a Katu warrior. Caine was still as skilled with a bow or lance as with an M-16 assault rifle. He frequently ventured into the forest alone and spent hours—or even days, if work permitted—with only a survival knife on his belt.

He ate what he could find: grass, bark, berries, roots, grubs, fish, whatever. He slept under the stars and honed his skills as a tracker, hunter, and camouflage expert. For Caine, this was necessary to maintain his sanity. He had to keep the Katu part of his personality alive because it had become as important to his nature as anything he had acquired from so-called civilized society or the military.

The rifle shots sounded close to the compound. Caine moved toward the shots, but realized the dense foliage would prevent him from seeing past the forest. He reached for the lower branches of a large Douglas fir and pulled himself upward. Caine braced his boots along the trunk and climbed higher, using branches for hand- and footholds.

Scaling the tree was as easy for Caine as climbing the rungs of a ladder. He ascended into the upper branches and used the elevated position to peer out above the smaller trees. Caine saw movement in a clearing beyond the compound. A large dark figure thrashed through the tall grass. The shaggy shape ran on all fours, its head raised with jaws parted to reveal great sharp teeth.

"Help!" a man's voice cried out. "Jesus . . . help . . . me . . ."

Caine climbed higher to get a better look at the scene below. He saw the man. An overweight guy dressed in a checkered shirt, baggy trousers, and a leather vest was running awkwardly away from the bear. His cry for help was choked off by labored gasps. The fleeing man carried a hunting rifle in his fist, but he made no attempt to use it against the charging beast.

Steve Caine was unarmed except for the survival knife on his belt. There was nothing he could do to help the unfortunate stranger. The bear was closing in fast and the guy didn't have a chance in hell of outrunning the angry carnivore. Caine noticed a crimson blotch on the bear's black fur: the hunter must have already shot it. The idiot was probably an irresponsible hunter—a fool who'd never learned to handle his rifle properly.

Caine despised such so-called hunters. They killed animals for trophies, not for food. They lacked the heart of
the true hunter, one who doesn't take life without good
reason and hones his skills to make the kill quick and clean.
Caine and the other members of the Hard Corps were all
hunters, and they upheld the code of decent conduct when
they hunted.

It was clear the moron outside the compound had violated
all the rules. He had fired at an animal he almost certainly
did not intend to eat. He had wounded the beast instead of
killing it. Apparently the turkey-butt had either run out of
ammunition or his weapon had jammed and he had been
too stupid to consider the fact the bear might attack. He'd
either failed to carry a backup piece and consider the possible
need for cover, or he had panicked. Either way, he was
about to pay for his mistakes with his life.

The bear lunged and pounced on the man. Claws and
teeth ripped into human flesh. The man's shrieks of terror
and agony echoed among the trees as the powerful carnivore
tore the incompetent hunter apart.

Caine had seen much suffering and death. The mercenary
did not feel much remorse for the slain hunter. He'd seen
too many innocent people, people who'd done nothing to
provoke their assailants, mutilated and murdered or vic-
timized. In fact, Caine felt more sympathy for the bear than
the man.

Once the kill was made, the beast headed howling toward
the compound. Animals aren't people. The bear didn't
understand the pain of the bullets in its flesh. It had killed
its attacker, yet the pain continued. The beast would certainly
strike out at anyone or anything it encountered.

The bellow of the wounded bear was nearly lost amid the
roar of rotor blades as a helicopter approached the compound. Caine glanced up at the pale morning sky, shielding
his eyes from the glare of the sun with the rim of his boonie
hat. It was the Bell UH-1D. The other three members of

the Hard Corps were returning to the compound—and the wounded bear was headed straight for the helicopter pad.

A chain-link fence surrounded the compound, but a portion of the fence near the helipad was down. It had been struck by lightning the night before and the alarm system built into the fence had been shorted out. Caine had helped John McShayne, the Hard Corps jack-of-all-trades, disconnect the damaged section. McShayne had intended to repair the wiring, but he didn't have what was needed to fix the alarm. Caine didn't understand electronics and whatever McShayne said on the subject made more sense than anything the merc warrior might think.

Caine smiled slightly as he climbed down the tree and dropped to the ground. The situation wasn't amusing, but Caine smiled at the irony that McShayne's decision to leave the fence down had left an open gate for the renegade bear.

John McShayne was the first sergeant at the Hard Corps compound. A thirty-year veteran of the United States Army, McShayne had seen action in Korea and Vietnam, but he was basically a behind-the-lines soldier. He was skilled as both a motor-pool mechanic and a helicopter repair expert. He had handled supply, personnel, payroll, filing, and bookkeeping. McShayne had been trained in computers and electronics.

After he'd retired from the military, McShayne had decided to join a different sort of army. He found out about the Hard Corps and met the mercenaries when they were recruiting guys for a mission in Central America. McShayne wanted to join. He admitted he was too old to be a grunt and really wasn't trained as a combat specialist like the Special Forces vets. But, McShayne could handle just about everything they needed behind the front lines. He became their "top" sergeant and took care of everything from records and communications to mess hall and baby-sitting the compound while the Hard Corps was gone on assignment.

McShayne was as vital to the success of the Hard Corps as any one of the original four members. Top was the unit "mother hen" who fussed over the men, grumbled about his work, but never let them down when they needed him. It was hard to believe the Hard Corps had ever been able to get along without him.

Yet, McShayne had a strange paranoia about bears. He was always worried that the bears were going to get into the compound and wreck the place. Occasionally, bears had entered the compound in the past. Basically shy and frightened by humans, the bears had been more a nuisance than a threat. But McShayne always insisted on carrying a .44 Magnum Smith & Wesson model 29 revolver in case he ever had to shoot one of those "big hairy bastards." The closest he'd ever come to this was when he'd found a female bear with two cubs, sitting in the garbage before the fence was completed. McShayne had fired his Magnum, but he'd only shot into the air to scare the animals away.

McShayne had probably gone to the pad to meet the chopper. The three men in the Bell whirlybird would be virtually unarmed. The noise from the chopper might conceal the bear's approach. If the bear hit the pad at the right moment, it was possible that one or more of the men would be killed or injured.

Caine grabbed a pole, a sturdy tree branch five feet long, which he had previously prepared as a walking stave. He had selected the stave because the end fitted in the hollow handle of his survival knife. He drew the knife as he ran toward the pad. Caine wished he had time to run to his quarters and get his rifle or even his bow and arrows. But he would have to make do with what he had.

The merc unscrewed the cap at the end of the knife handle and shook out the contents. Some survival gear was stored in the handle—fishing line, hooks and sinkers, some matches, and a wire saw, which could serve as a garrote. Caine pocketed all the items except the fishing line.

He continued to run as he jammed the end of the pole into the hollow knife handle. Caine stopped briefly to ram the butt of the stave into the trunk of a tree to make certain the pole was firmly in place. Then he wound the line tightly around the handle and secured it to the shaft. The improvised spear was ready and Caine continued to head for the helicopter pad.

The Bell chopper set down slowly. McShayne was waiting for it, standing near the airstrip. As Caine had feared, no one noticed the bear as it charged through the gap in the fence.

Caine ran up, scooped up a rock the size of a man's skull, and hurled it at the bear. The stone struck the animal just under the left ear. The bear roared with rage and spun about to face Caine.

The creature's speed and agility were remarkable considering its great size. Caine waved his arms to get the bear's attention, swinging the spear in his fist. He felt as if he were signaling for a hairy version of the Grim Reaper to come and get him. The bear seemed eager to accept the offer and charged.

Caine dashed to a pair of slender hemlock trees set less than a yard apart with a thick tree stump behind them. He waited for the bear to draw closer, his heart throbbing wildly as he realized the dreadful risk involved. He had to time his move perfectly. If he failed, Caine wouldn't get another chance and he'd probably end up no better off than the moronic hunter.

The beast was closing in fast and prepared to lunge. Caine jumped between the hemlocks and jammed the butt of the spear against the base of the tree stump. He held the shaft high, knife blade pointed at the bear. The animal rose to full height when it reached the V-shaped hemlocks. It was nearly seven feet tall and to Steve Caine the bear looked as big as a mountain.

Great paws with dagger claws struck out at Caine. He

dropped to one knee and held the spear in place. The bear
hit the lance. The shaft snapped like a toothpick under the
strain of the beast's weight. A terrible howl erupted as the
bear clawed at the hemlocks, raking off long strips of bark.

Caine glanced up at the bear. Half the spear remained in
the animal's chest. The six-inch blade and handguard of the
handle was buried in the dense black fur. The bear weaved
slightly and crashed to the ground. The blade had lanced
the creature's heart. It died very quickly.

"Jesus Christ!" McShayne exclaimed as he approached,
the big .44 Magnum revolver in his fist. "What the hell
happened?"

"Thought you might like a bearskin rug, Top," Caine
replied. His calm voice concealed the enormous stress he'd
experienced from the ordeal.

"Holy shit," Joe Fanelli remarked as the other three
mercs arrived from the chopper. "You killed this thing with
a *spear*?"

"It was all I could come up with on such short notice,"
Caine confessed. He stepped around the bear, still half-
expecting the beast to rise up and attack once more. "So,
how did things go in New York?"

"Sort of similar to your situation here," William O'Neal
replied, glancing down at the fur-covered carcass. "Hairy."

CHAPTER 4

JOHN MCSHAYNE MUTTERED something about "goddamn bears" as he carried a tray of coffee mugs to a table in the mess hall. The top sergeant was built rather like a bear himself. He was a big man with a barrel chest and thick limbs. In his late fifties, McShayne was still more fit than men half his age. He placed the tray on the table and sat with the four Hard Corps mercs.

"Okay, fellas," O'Neal began after explaining the mission to Caine. "Zabibu is going back to Africa tonight. We've got to let him know whether or not we're taking the job."

"We don't have anything lined up," Caine said with a shrug. "Let's do it."

"Figure you can bear it, huh?" Fanelli said with a smile.

"Before we forget," O'Neal declared as he turned to McShayne, "contact the forest rangers and tell them to come get the body of that shithead hunter who got mauled to death by the bear. We'll have to let 'em in so they can examine the critter and confirm that the animal killed him. Let 'em know the bear is dead and it can't hurt anybody again.''

"When they arrive you might tell them we don't want any publicity about how the bear was killed or who did it," Wentworth added. "After all, *Man Kills Rampaging Bear With Spear* is just begging to be a headline for the evening news."

"I'll take care of it," McShayne confirmed with a nod. "Oh, Saintly called while you were gone. I think he suspects you guys were involved in that shoot-out in New York. He didn't sound too happy."

"He never does," O'Neal said with a sigh.

"Saintly" was Joshua St. Laurent, the case officer with the Central Intelligence Agency. St. Laurent spent most of his time with CIA operations in Ottawa, Canada. "Old Saintly"—as the Hard Corps called him—kept in touch with the mercenaries because the Company occasionally needed the services of soldiers of fortune to deal with certain covert actions that the government didn't want to be directly associated with.

The relationship was a two-way street because the Hard Corps benefited from their association with Saintly. The guy helped to keep Uncle Sam off their ass. The Hard Corps didn't pay taxes and they had violated all sorts of BATF regulations, housing laws, and probably dozens of other federal rules they didn't even know about. St. Laurent and the Company steered the other Feds away from the Hard Corps. Saintly also shared some classified information with the mercenaries—when it suited the interests of the Company, sometimes provided them with perks, such as those pass cards that had helped at Kennedy Airport, which they had kept from an earlier occasion, and every once in a while even hired them for a mission.

There were also disadvantages in this relationship. Saintly

could use information about the mercenaries to blackmail them into cooperating with the Company. The Hard Corps had access to sources of information that the CIA, the National Security Agency, and other federal organizations weren't privy to. But Saintly was smart enough not to push the mercenaries, aware the Hard Corps could simply leave the compound and set up a new base of operations elsewhere. He seldom pressured the mercs to cooperate with the CIA or supply information against their will.

"Okay," O'Neal began, lighting a cigarette as he reached for a cup of coffee with his other hand. "I'll contact Saintly. The rest of you guys get ready to pull out. Pack civilian clothes, cameras, tourist junk."

"Excuse me, sir," Caine said as he held a cup in both hands, as if relishing the warmth of the coffee. "I assume you've considered the fact that whoever arranged the ambush in New York knew enough about Zabibu to arrange the reception. They knew what city he'd be in, probably what hotel he had reservations for, and which route he'd probably take to get there. They may also have known why he was in America, when the government and even the media didn't know, which means they might already know about us."

"That's unlikely," Wentworth stated, placing his fingertips together to form a small tent with his hands. "Jacob was in New York to meet other people besides us. It was top secret, for sure. But his country needs money, lots of it. If his visit hadn't been cut short, he had some very promising financial connections lined up. Now, the gang that ambushed us had just robbed a jewelry store, and supposedly, they were trying to get away and hit our van by accident. That's the story. Since all the bad guys are dead, including the gunmen who shot down some cops, the police are willing to overlook some of the holes in that story—such as why the jewel thieves were backed up by three extra gunmen who appeared from nowhere."

"How did Zabibu explain how he wound up with you

guys and why you all happened to have guns?'' McShayne asked. "I understand the cops take a dim view of people running around with guns and gettin' in public shoot-outs.''

"Zabibu claimed one of his bodyguards had arranged for security when he arrived in New York," Fanelli answered, finishing the cup of coffee before lighting up a cigarette. ''He didn't know the bodyguard had contacted some mysterious bunch of gun-totin' guys who'd meet him at the airport and wind up shootin' it out with the so-called robbers. I don't think the cops really believe a word of it, but they're willing to let the matter slide as long as Zabibu gets the fuck outa New York as soon as possible.''

"What matters is the hit team failed," O'Neal commented, staring down at his coffee cup. "What bothers me is the attempt was really elaborate, and probably pretty expensive. Somebody went to a lot of trouble to try to off Zabibu and make it look like a freaky street crime without any political links. I don't think the Zaire government could have gone to such drastic measures to get rid of Zabibu. I doubt if the Angolans did it either. Even if they'd wanted to kill Zabibu while he was in New York, I don't think they could have put together a hit team of American low-life on such short notice.''

"I agree," Wentworth stated with a nod. "It had to be somebody with a well-organized intelligence network that already has agents operating within the United States. Somebody who also wants to get rid of Jacob Zabibu and the Republic of Kilembe. The Soviets have a strong interest in the region. They've been trying to expand their real estate in Africa for the last three decades. I figure the KGB arranged the hit.''

"Maybe," O'Neal said as he gulped down the last of his coffee. "It seemed a little sloppy for the KGB. Hiring street thugs to kill somebody doesn't seem like the style a *Morkrie Dela* assassin would use. Still, I won't argue with your point, Jim. The Soviets are probably involved somehow.

We might find ourselves up against some pretty bad odds when we get to Africa.''

"The Russian bear don't scare us.'' Fanelli grinned as he looked at Caine. "Just make sure you bring your knife, Steve.''

"That reminds me,'' O'Neal began as he rose from his chair. "Get that fence repaired before we get any more visitors. Okay, Top?''

"Yessir,'' McShayne replied. He turned to Fanelli and Caine. "Well, you heard the captain. Let's get to work.''

O'Neal left the mess hall and headed for the head shed. He entered the headquarters building. The orderly room was McShayne's main station. Desks with computers and radio transceivers were set up for the first sergeant's use in handling communications, data gathering, bookkeeping, and other duties. O'Neal spent so little time in the orderly room he sometimes felt as if he should ask McShayne's permission before he used it.

The Hard Corps commander sat at a radio set and turned the dial to the current frequency being monitored by Saintly's CIA station in Canada. A radio operator answered his call.

"This is Deep Six lookin' for my insurance man,'' O'Neal announced into the handset. "Is Mister Wonderful on duty?''

"I don't feel like listening to any of your feeble attempts at humor, Six,'' the familiar voice of Joshua St. Laurent replied. "I'm not very happy with you right now.''

"Did I forget our anniversary again?'' O'Neal asked in a bewildered tone. "I'll send you a gift later. What do you need? Another cloak or a new dagger?''

"I don't need any more Big Apple incidents,'' Saintly said in a hard voice. "Don't pretend you don't know what I'm talking about. My sources are reliable and I recognize your handiwork, Six. That could have caused a lot of trouble for all of us.''

"It really wasn't our fault, pal,'' O'Neal told him. "But

I can't explain that right now. By the way, we'll be gone for a while. You won't have to worry about us causing any domestic incidents for at least four months.''

"Really?'' Saintly replied. "That doesn't especially surprise me. I think I know where you're going, Six. I advise against it. Weather is pretty nasty this time of year.''

O'Neal frowned. He wasn't sure if St. Laurent was warning him to stay away from the mission because it was too risky, or because it would be contrary to the interests of the United States.

"Is this advice strongly motivated?'' O'Neal inquired.

"Just my personal opinion,'' the CIA case officer replied, which suggested Uncle Sam wouldn't object to the mission. "My opinion is based on what a friend of mine told me about his visit there. Weather is very bad and getting worse.''

"I see,'' O'Neal said, aware that Saintly was telling him that the CIA had already taken an interest in Kilembe. "I hope your friend didn't catch a bad cold.''

"He's still in pretty good health,'' Saintly answered, letting O'Neal know the CIA contacts hadn't been killed. "He was certainly glad to get home. By the way, he left an umbrella back there. A green umbrella. If you find it, my friend won't object if you use it while you're there.''

"Thank you,'' O'Neal smiled. An umbrella suggested something used for protection. Green meant it was used by the Army. The CIA must have smuggled in a clandestine shipment of arms to the Republic of Kilembe to help combat the terrorists. "I appreciate the advice. I really mean it.''

"Probably more than you deserve,'' St. Laurent replied. "My personal opinion is still the same. You're a fool if you plan to spend any time there. Guess that explains why you're going.''

"Guess so,'' O'Neal agreed. "Thanks again and I'll call you when I get back.''

"*If* you get back,'' the CIA contact replied grimly.

CHAPTER 5

LUIS PEREZ WISHED someone would pull the plug to the jukebox in the shabby little bar off Dupont Circle. A man dressed in a straw cowboy hat and ornate leather boots had fed about three dollars in quarters into the machine and punched up all the country-and-western records on the jukebox. Perez hated that sort of music. First Dolly Parton. Then Kenny Rogers. Then Dolly and Kenny together. Perez wished he'd brought along a pair of earplugs.

The Cuban wondered if someone had selected this shit-kicker tavern for the meeting as a sneaky way of punishing him because his plan had failed in New York. Many of the best restaurants in Washington, D.C., were on Dupont Circle, but Havana had decided he should wait for his control officer in a seedy little place with beer-guzzling yahoos.

He turned back to his beer and nursed it, thinking of the six years he had spent in Angola. He had gone there to instruct the Angolans in guerrilla warfare. Yet he had been frustrated by the difficulty in teaching them advanced techniques of sabotage and assassination. He decided this was because they had been poorly educated by the colonialist Portuguese. Actually, Perez had been a poor instructor, and short-tempered with his students. Beating a man with a bamboo cane teaches him little except fear and pain. Perez had also been inclined to think anyone who spoke Portuguese ought to be able to understand anything he said in Spanish. The fact he had trouble understanding Angolans who spoke Portuguese did not alter his opinion. As for those who spoke local tribal tongues, Perez dismissed them as hopeless morons.

Luis Perez spoke English and Russian fluently, yet he'd been sent to Africa along with more than twenty thousand other Cuban troops. The work hadn't been easy, and Perez had been glad to return to Cuba. He didn't mind being sent to the United States on a special UN Mission after all this. At least he spoke the language and he didn't have to spend every damn day in a country that couldn't even feed itself. Then he learned the reason for his new assignment. General Zabibu had planned a trip to the United States and Perez was supposed to terminate the troublesome officer with extreme prejudice.

The hit had been thrown together rather quickly, but Perez had thought the scheme was inspired at the time he conceived it. American hoodlums would be used: petty criminals who free-lanced as strong-arm goons for the protection rackets and cocaine trafficking in New York City. The hit wouldn't appear to be a political assassination and the Republic of Kilembe would have no one to point an accusing finger at except the United States of America in general and the alarming crime rate of New York City in particular.

Now the plan had failed. The Cuban G-2 Department wasn't known for being understanding toward failures. Perez tried not to think about what G-2 might decide to do to him. He ordered another beer and returned to his table at the rear of the room. Perez sat with his back to the wall as he sipped the foamy brew and waited.

Twenty minutes passed before a short fat man dressed in soiled chinos and a Hawaiian shirt entered the bar. His skin was dark and sweat stained his armpits and shirtfront. A blue baseball cap with "D.C." printed in yellow letters above the bill was perched on his head, and light flashed along the gold band of the Rolex watch on his wrist. He placed his flat leather valise under his arm as he smiled at the bartender and ordered a beer.

"Hey, Miguel!" the fat man greeted and waved at Perez. "I see you made it after all."

"I made it," Perez replied with a nod as the man approached his table. "I was beginning to wonder if you forgot about me."

"Nobody's going to forget about you for a while," the fat man commented as he sat across the table from Perez.

He stared at Perez's hard, lean face. Perez was an athletic man who had yet to see his fortieth birthday. His eyes were dark, almost black, and the lines of his mouth suggested he seldom smiled. Many women had found Luis Perez very attractive. Women in Havana, in Washington, in Luanda had been drawn to this man who never talked much about his work. Few suspected the reason was because he was in the business of killing people and teaching others how to kill.

Perez stroked his pencil-thin black mustache with his left index finger. His right hand rested in his lap under the table. He carried a small .25 auto pistol in an ankle holster and a spring-loaded stiletto strapped to his forearm. He didn't think he'd need either weapon, but he didn't assume he was safe simply because the meeting was in a public place.

"Your efforts in New York were very clumsy, my dear colleague," the fat man whispered softly in Spanish. "We are less than happy with you back home. However, at least your bungled plan didn't implicate our government at all. In that, you're fortunate."

"I might even have been successful if I hadn't been ordered to come back to Washington instead of remaining in New York," Perez stated. "I could still have killed Zabibu.

An airplane crash perhaps. Find out what flight he would be on for his return to Africa and slip in an explosive surprise among the baggage—"

"No," the control officer told him. "If anything happens to Zabibu now, his country will certainly demand an investigation."

"So what?" Perez said with a smile. "Let them fish about in the Atlantic Ocean for the wreckage. They wouldn't be able to prove anything."

"But they could get the sympathy and support of the United States and other NATO countries," the fat man stated. "That could lead to more trouble than Zabibu is worth. We want him and the others in that government of traitors dealt with quickly. And completely."

"So . . . more terrorist attacks? Cutting off trade routes?" Perez asked. "I think that's an effective method and one which will certainly wear them down. I doubt if they can last eight months—"

"We don't want them to last half that long," the control agent declared as he unzipped his valise. "I have something for you. Can you guess what it is?"

"An airline ticket," Perez replied with a sigh. He wasn't guessing. He knew what G-2 had in mind. "Probably a passport and other identification under a new name. Correct?"

"*¡Muy bien!*" The fat man smiled. "And I suppose you've also guessed that you'll be going back to Angola. Leading political revolutionaries in special operations was your specialty. You're getting an honorary promotion to full colonel. Isn't that wonderful news?"

"*Sí,*" Perez said without enthusiasm. "And why am I receiving this great honor?"

"Because you're going to personally supervise the attacks on Kilembe," the control agent explained.

"I understand," Perez assured him.

"Then you also understand that you'd better succeed this

time," the G-2 contact remarked as he handed a thick packet
of materials to Perez. "If you succeed you'll be promoted
to field-grade officer and given your choice of your next
duty station. If you fail . . . well, I think you know what
will happen then."

"Tell your superiors I'll take care of everything," Perez
answered, stuffing the packet inside his jacket. "Now, get
out of my sight, you fat lazy pig."

The control agent stiffened, but he did not respond to the
insult. He was a paper pusher and realized Perez could cut
him to pieces if he tried to get physical with the experienced
and potentially dangerous field operative. The contact man
simply rose from his chair and marched from the tavern.
Perez smiled, pleased with his minor victory.

"Hey, taco boy!" A tall lanky man in a cowboy hat, a
checkered shirt with pearl buttons, and a pair of denim pants
approached Perez's table. "You and yore buddy reckon on
doin' business in town?"

"Don't worry," Perez replied and rose to his feet. "I'm
leaving right now and I don't want any trouble."

"Then you'll just get yore greasy little ass out that door
over thar," the cowboy declared. Another man appeared
behind him. The second man was shorter than the cowboy,
but thickly built with plenty of muscle mixed in with a layer
of fat. "We's gonna have a talk, boy."

Perez glanced at the other patrons along the bar. None
of them so much as glanced over a shoulder at him and the
two hillbilly bullies. The bartender was suddenly very interested in washing beer mugs—an activity he hadn't seemed
to care about since Perez had entered this dump. Obviously,
they didn't want to get involved in whatever the yahoos
were up to.

The Cuban realized there was no point in expecting any
help from the bartender and the conveniently deaf, dumb,
and blind patrons. Perez would have to handle the two
clowns on his own and he didn't care to have any witnesses

anyway. He decided the best choice of action was simply to go along with the cowboys' demands.

He obeyed instructions and walked to the back door. The two cowboys followed. The lanky guy reached down and drew a hunting knife from his boot while his partner slipped a set of brass knuckledusters onto his right fist. Perez opened the door and one of the thugs pushed him into the narrow alley outside. The Cuban grunted as he landed against a brick wall.

"Don't get cute or I'll cut you open," the lanky man announced as he grabbed Perez's lapel and held the blade of his knife in front of the Cuban's face. "Me and Leon don't take kindly to you gawddamn Mexicans and Colombians musclin' in on our racket."

Leon muttered something in agreement with his partner as he closed the door and stood behind his buddy. Perez raised his hands in surrender as the first man shoved his back against the wall.

"If'n there's gonna be any nose candy gettin' sold in this town we're gonna be doin' it, boy," the cowboy snorted as he held the knife at Perez's face and slipped his other hand inside the Cuban's jacket. "You jerks got a lotta nerve to make a cocaine deal right under our noses."

"We won't do it again," Perez assured him.

"What we got here?" the hood wondered out loud as he took the packet from Perez's pocket. "Money, or dope?"

"Death," Perez hissed in reply.

His left hand suddenly seized the man's wrist and twisted it to turn the hunting knife away from his face. Perez's right hand snapped forward and the stiletto appeared in his palm. A single stroke of the razor-sharp five-inch blade sliced open the hoodlum's throat. The cowboy dropped his knife as blood gushed across his fancy checkered shirt.

Perez shoved his opponent backward to crash into the second hoodlum. Leon pushed his dying partner to the ground and raised his brass-knuckled fist. Perez wasn't impressed. He flashed the stiletto to get the goon's attention and swiftly launched a karate roundhouse kick to his opponent's face.

Leon's jawbone shattered and he fell to the ground. Perez descended on the fallen thug and thrust the point of his stiletto under the man's sternum. The blade pierced the solar plexus at an upward angle to stab deep into the heart. Perez yanked up the dying man's shirt to keep most of the blood from splashing his own clothing.

"*¡Estúpidos cabrones!*" the Cuban rasped as he wiped the blood from his blade, using Leon's pant leg.

He watched Leon's body twitch for the last time and gathered up the packet that the lanky stooge had taken from him. Perez returned it to his jacket and slid the stiletto up his right sleeve until he heard a click; the weapon was securely locked in place on the spring-loaded lever strapped to his forearm.

The Cuban glanced up the alley. No one stood at the entrance and traffic moved along at a regular pace. There had been no witnesses. He paused for a moment to spit into the lifeless face of the rawboned goon who had insulted and manhandled him.

Then Luis Perez strolled calmly from the alley and headed up the street.

CHAPTER 6

THERE WERE NO commercial airline flights to the Republic of Kilembe. The Hard Corps had to settle for a flight to Zaire instead. They arrived at Ndjili International Airport near Kinshasa. The mercenaries' false identification papers and passports easily passed customs. They retrieved their luggage and rented a Toyota van.

Kinshasa is one of the more modern cities of Zaire. The construction of buildings and streets reflects a strong European influence, a legacy of the country's former identity as the Belgian Congo. The same can be said of the street signs and legends written in French. Many signs are also written in English. Only a few include translations in Swahili, Lingala, Tshiluba, or Kikongo, although these African languages are spoken by millions of Zaïrois.

Traffic was light and the Toyota had no trouble making its way through the pitted and tar-patched streets. A few hotels, office buildings, and government structures were tall modern buildings of concrete and steel. However, smaller stores, restaurants, and assorted shops comprised the majority of the buildings. Sidewalk cafes appeared to be quite popular, and the Hard Corps passed several churches, most of which seemed to be Roman Catholic.

The ubiquitous street merchants and children lining the roads were intrigued by the sight of four white guys driving along in a van with baggage piled in the back. Tourists are much sought-after in Zaire, which doesn't enjoy the profitable benefits of the major tourism of Kenya, Morocco, or South Africa. The merchants waved wood carvings of animals and "genuine ritual masks." When the Toyota stopped at a light, hawkers offered to sell jewelry or novelty items at an "incredibly low price." A lot of these guys were impressive linguists, able to deliver a fast-talking sales pitch in four or five languages. The street kids were even better. Skinny and filthy, they were asking for handouts in French, English, Spanish, German, and Italian. Without missing a beat, they also offered to wash the car, carry luggage, or guide the four men around Kinshasa. And one kid even volunteered his sister for sexual pleasures at a very low price.

"How old is she, kid?" Fanelli inquired.

"Oh, for God's sake!" Wentworth exclaimed, disgusted by Fanelli's question. "I think you'd screw a wildebeest if somebody'd hold it still for you."

"We talkin' about a *female* wildebeest, Lieutenant?" Fanelli asked with mock sincerity.

"Knock it off," O'Neal growled, examining a map of the area. "Keep going east until we're out of the city."

"Okay," Fanelli replied, concentrating on driving the Toyota. "Then what?"

"See this road? We go as far as Kikwit, then turn south until we reach the Kilembe border," O'Neal instructed, folding up the map.

"Gee, thanks," Fanelli muttered sourly.

"Just keep following this road," O'Neal repeated.

"We're bound to find the border eventually."

"We're heading the right way right now," Caine stated as he checked a shock-resistant compass built into the butt of his survival knife.

"Any idea how many kilometers we'll have to travel to get there?" Wentworth asked as he pulled a camouflage-print beret onto his head. "Perhaps I should look at the map—"

"Kilembe isn't on the map," O'Neal explained. "We have to sort of guess where it is."

"I sure hope we've got a full tank of gas," Fanelli commented as he checked the gauge. "We just might need it."

The Toyota rolled on out of Kinshasa, heading east, away from the Congo River and toward the Republic of Kilembe. The weather was hot and humid, not unlike New York City had been the previous week.

The scenery outside the city changed dramatically. Forests of mahogany, ebony, and African cedar lined the rutted gravel-covered road. A truck appeared from the opposite direction. The dark face of the driver smiled at the mercenaries as the vehicles passed. Two young men rode in the back of the vehicle along with almost a ton of bananas. The laborers cheerfully waved at the mercs and tossed them a bunch of the fruit, which Caine caught before he waved back.

"An airmail lunch," he remarked, handing bananas to his partners.

"Wonder why they gave us these things?" Wentworth remarked, a trace of suspicion in his voice.

"They're probably just in a good mood because they're taking a truckload of bananas to market," O'Neal told his paranoid second-in-command. "Just enjoy the gift."

The Toyota passed a small rubber plantation, where workers were busy sawing down larger, mature trees. The plantation personnel didn't look as pleased as the men in the truck had. They simply stopped their work to stare at the passing van.

The mercenaries now drove along a river, one of the tributaries of the Kasai. Villages dotted the terrain. Some were little more than collections of crude huts where Nilotic tribes lived as their ancestors had for centuries. These primitive people, clad in loincloths and handmade jewelry of stones, metals, and bone, watched the Toyota pass by their village with little interest. They obviously knew the twentieth century existed beyond their village, but chose to ignore it.

The Toyota came to the frontier—a small, pockmarked stucco building under a baking sun, and a few tense-looking guards pacing behind a red-and-white barrier. Beyond the guards, the mercs could see a row of jeeps and trucks, and other military personnel.

"*Bonjour, messieurs,*" Wentworth greeted two grim-faced guards. "*Qu'est-ce qu'il y a?*" he asked, pointing at the barrier.

"*L'entrée, maintenant, c'est interdite,*" one of the guards stated, showing no interest in seeing passports. "*Vous ne pouvez pas entrer, monsieur.*"

"What's wrong?" O'Neal asked his second-in-command.

"They won't let us through," Wentworth answered. "Looks like Zaire's decided to close the border with Kilembe."

"Shit," Fanelli muttered with disgust. "What do we do now?"

"Back up and get out of here," O'Neal replied. "Everybody nod and wave at the troopers so they know we're not gonna be a problem."

Wentworth turned back to the guardsmen, who were now looking downright hostile. "*Bien. Il n'y a rien, messieurs. Merci. Au revoir.*"

Fanelli backed up the Toyota and turned the vehicle away from the border. O'Neal pulled back his sleeve and checked his watch. The sky suggested it would be dusk in about an hour. Maybe sooner. Twilight often falls abruptly around the equator.

"Okay, guys," the Hard Corps commander began. "We're gonna have to sneak across the border after dark. Any suggestions?"

"Get off the road and search for a portion of the border that isn't well guarded," Caine replied. "An area with dense vegetation for cover."

"Might be able to arrange a nice distraction, too," Fanelli added with a sly grin. "There's gotta be somethin' around here I can blow up."

"Just be careful you don't blow up a Zaire trooper in the process," O'Neal told him. "These guys may look like trouble, but they aren't the enemy and we don't wanna hurt any of 'em."

"It would be nice if we could count on them feeling the same way about us," Wentworth said with a sigh.

The Hard Corps abandoned the van roughly two miles from the border. They trekked slowly back to the frontier, each carrying a backpack with some fundamental items from their luggage. The gear they carried in the packs varied according to each man's individual tastes, but all carried extra underwear and socks, a toothbrush, and extra tubes of toothpaste. Each man also carried a first-aid kit, canteen, binoculars, a rain poncho, and some rations.

They had no firearms. O'Neal carried a machete and Caine had his trusted survival knife. Wentworth had found a straight tree limb, about three-and-a-half-feet long, to use as an improvised stave. The only weapon Fanelli carried was an entrenching tool with a folding handle and a steel shovel blade, sharpened on the edges. The tool could serve as an improvised battle-ax in an emergency, a trick he'd learned in Vietnam.

The empty soft-drink bottle Fanelli carried wasn't intended for use as a weapon. The bottle wasn't really "empty" since he'd replaced the original contents with damp soil and gasoline siphoned from the fuel tank of the Toyota. A twisted rag stuffed in the mouth of the bottle would serve as a fuse for the makeshift explosive.

Darkness, as O'Neal had expected, descended rapidly. It was completely dark by the time the Hard Corps reached the border. They favored the brush areas and moved in the concealment of tall grass, giant ferns, and clusters of trees. Vines dangled from limbs and twisted roots threatened to snag a boot with every step.

Night birds called in the darkness and the voices of thousands of tree frogs and chirping insects added to the chorus. In the distance, some kind of cat roared. Probably a leopard, O'Neal thought, recalling what little he knew about African wildlife. Lions favor the open plains and savannahs. Leopards dwell in jungles and hunt alone at night. He seemed to recall reading that leopards were also more apt to attack human beings than any of the other big cats. He hoped he remembered that wrong.

Lots of insects bit the four Hard Corps mercs as they crept through the jungle toward the border. They couldn't even swat the tiny bloodsuckers because the sound might alert the guards. The mercs could only hope the insects didn't carry any nasty parasite and all the bites would cause was a little swelling.

Leopards and strange insects aside, man remained the greatest enemy for the Hard Corps. Although Zaïrois border guards were positioned along the frontier, there were no actual fences or walls off the roads to divide Zaire from Kilembe.

The mercenaries found a site with plenty of cover and only eight guards patrolling a mile-long stretch of the border. O'Neal selected a point to cross and indicated the spot with an index finger. The others nodded in agreement. The Hard Corps leader gestured for Caine to go forward. Fanelli placed a hand on O'Neal's arm. The wiry Italian-American held the bottle-bomb in his fist and jerked his head to the right. O'Neal nodded.

Fanelli shuffled quietly away from the others. He moved about a hundred yards to the north and ducked behind an oil palm. Fanelli used his entrenching tool to pry a large stone from the ground. He smiled thinly as he eased the bottle under the rock with the neck and fuse jutting out.

Joe Fanelli was the team demolitions expert. He had used all sorts of explosives, everything from RDX plastique to makeshift explosives with batshit as the main ingredient. Fanelli liked working with explosives. He enjoyed the special sense of power he felt from being able to demolish something with a great big bang. The bottle-bomb wouldn't be overly loud, though.

Fanelli pushed some dirt and smaller rocks around the bottle to contain the blast. He didn't want flaming gasoline to set the jungle on fire. Satisfied, he flicked the wheel of his cigarette lighter and set the flame to the rag fuse.

Fanelli rushed back to O'Neal and Wentworth. Caine had already ventured forward, blending into the shadows as if he were part of the natural environment. He approached the border like a cat, creeping on all fours, testing each move with palm, knee, or foot before putting full weight on a limb. His body slithered below the tips of grass and he breathed silently through parted lips. Caine inhaled and exhaled in steady even breaths, aware even this sound could give him away if he wasn't careful. The controlled breath helped control his movements. It helped control the fear.

But Caine couldn't control the insects and tree frogs. The creatures sensed his approach and ceased chirping. The sudden silence might warn the guards that danger was near. Caine wondered if any of the Zaïrois troops had noticed.

Suddenly the bottle exploded. The gasoline in the container had been carefully packed with mud to serve as a buffer without watering down the flammable liquid. The blast wasn't very impressive, although the rocks sailed into the trees and flames burst into being.

Perfect, O'Neal thought, pleased with Fanelli's handiwork. *A nice little distraction. Just what we need. No more, no less.*

"Feu!" an excited guard cried out as he pointed at

the blaze. He repeated the warning in Swahili. *"Moto!"*

"Où est-il?" another guard demanded before he saw where the man was pointing. *"Merde alors! Feu!"*

"Pa-le moto!" a third guard exclaimed as several soldiers ran toward the fire to extinguish the blaze.

Only two guards remained at the immediate position where the Hard Corps intended to cross the border. Both men remained at their post as they stared at the troops who had rushed forward to deal with the mysterious fire. Steve Caine rose silently behind one of the sentries and hit him hard behind the ear with the butt of his survival knife. The man uttered a half grunt, half sigh, and wilted senseless to the ground.

The second guard turned to face Caine. His face expressed raw terror as he fumbled with the shoulder strap to his rifle and tried to unsling his M-16. Suddenly, three more figures appeared from the bush and dashed straight toward him.

He didn't know which opponent to deal with first, so he simply followed instinct and swung the rifle toward Steve Caine, who appeared to be his nearest attacker. The man gasped with surprise when he discovered Caine no longer stood before him. He had only taken his eyes off the tall bearded white man for a split second. How could he vanish so quickly?

Too late, the sentry turned his attention back to the other three Hard Corps warriors. Wentworth reached the man first and struck out with his improvised stave. The hardwood pole cracked against the guard's forearms and jarred the M-16 from his grasp. Wentworth quickly reversed his grip on the stick and jabbed an end into the guard's abdomen.

The guardsman doubled up with a gasp and Wentworth adroitly slipped the end of his stave under the man's right armpit. The merc lieutenant grabbed the man's right wrist with one hand and easily twisted the Zaïrois's arm behind his back, using the shaft of the stick for additional leverage.

Wentworth stepped behind his opponent and stamped a boot into the back of the guy's knee. The guard's leg buckled and he fell to his knees while Wentworth maintained the hammerlock with the stave braced under the man's bent elbow and anchored between his shoulder blades.

"Hapana, mtu!" the guard pleaded in rapid Swahili. *"Tafadhali, hapana—"*

Wentworth suddenly released the man and swiftly chopped the side of a hand into the nerve center of the guard's neck muscle. The Zaïrois lost consciousness and fell face-first on the ground.

Steve Caine rose beside the senseless figure of the other guard. The stealthful merc's disappearing act had been a simple feat. He had taken advantage of the other guard's distraction when his three fellow mercs had arrived, and had dropped to the ground behind the motionless shape of the first sentry. No magic, just an unexpected technique.

"Good work, gentlemen," O'Neal declared as he scooped up the second guard's M-16 rifle.

"As always, Captain," Fanelli replied cheerfully.

Caine had already taken the other guard's rifle and spare magazines for the weapon. Wentworth relieved the second man of the mags from his ammo pouches as well. The four mercenaries hurried across the border before the rest of the Zaire guard force realized what had happened. Outraged voices shouted in French, Swahili, and Lingala, but no shots were fired. The Hard Corps had vanished into the jungle on the opposite side of the border.

They were now in the Republic of Kilembe.

CHAPTER 7

"I WAS AFRAID you might not get across," General Zabibu declared as he shook hands with the four mercenaries. "I should have guessed Kinshasa might try something like that."

"But Zaire didn't try to stop you from returning to Kilembe?" O'Neal inquired as he accepted a balloon glass of brandy from Zabibu.

"Too much publicity," the general said with a smile. He poured some more brandy and handed a glass to James Wentworth. "We've got UPI nosing about. Zaire would *love* to arrest me, or shoot me while I'm in Zaire. But the government *can't* arrest me, even if it does think I'm a traitor. Zaire is worried about world opinion. Bad press has already hurt its relations with the Western democracies, and any more might hurt the foreign aid it receives."

"*Merci, mon vieux,*" Wentworth said as he took the glass. "I wouldn't count too much on protection by the press. We didn't see any reporters on our way in.''

"Perhaps not," Zabibu replied as he prepared another glass of brandy. "But I still think I'm safe from any rash actions by the Zaire government. They know about the assassination attempt in New York. They don't want anything to happen to me when I'm in their country."

He offered the glass to Fanelli. The tough Italian from Jersey sighed and shook his head. Fanelli was a recovering alcoholic. After he'd returned from Vietnam and discovered veterans of that conflict were being treated like lepers, Fanelli had retreated into a bottle for more than a year. O'Neal and Wentworth had found him in a VA detox center when they were putting together the new Hard Corps as a mercenary unit.

That had been more than ten years ago. Fanelli had been on the wagon ever since. He'd slipped a couple of times, but he'd only really fucked up once. That had been during a mission in Bolivia a while back. Fanelli had wound up in jail and his partners broke him out. He could have gotten himself or the other members of the team killed by his carelessness.

"No thanks, General," he told Zabibu, not bothering to explain why.

The general sure looks different than he did back in New York, Fanelli mused. Zabibu wore a short-sleeve khaki shirt and trousers. The uniform reflected the influence America had imprinted on Zabibu's personality. He wore a silver star on each collar and one on his garrison cap. Only three or four ribbons and a winged-parachute emblem of a paratrooper were pinned to his shirt. Most African generals wear so many medals hanging from their chests they resemble walking Christmas trees.

Zabibu wasn't a show-off or a hypocrite. His office was simple, with a desk, two armchairs, and a bookcase. The brandy seemed to be the only notable luxury that the rest of the troops didn't enjoy. From the expression on O'Neal's face, Fanelli guessed the brandy wasn't all that great anyway.

"Would you care for this drink, then?" Zabibu asked Steve Caine as he held out the balloon glass.

"Maybe after the mission is over," Caine replied. "Thanks anyway."

"Comme vous voudrez," the general said with a shrug as he placed the glass on his desk. "Sorry about slipping into French like that. It is my first language and I still think in French. You know? I'm going to try harder to think in English. After all, it is the official language of the Republic of Kilembe."

"English?" Fanelli asked with surprise.

"English is the official language of many African nations, my friend," Zabibu explained. "The Gambia, Botswana, Ghana. Nigeria, Liberia, Zambia, and Zimbabwe. Maybe some others I forgot. Of course, most of our citizens don't yet speak English, but we don't have a common language among Kilembans. They speak French, Swahili, Portuguese, a dozen other languages. Still, English will serve our country better than any other language."

"If you last that long," O'Neal commented, finishing his brandy. "I don't want to sound negative, General, but we've had to play hide-and-seek with the border patrol and then wander about in the goddamn jungle until we found our way to your contacts at the road. One of 'em almost took a shot at us before we managed to tell him who we were. It's been a long fuckin' night."

"Of course," Zabibu said with a nod. "I apologize for rambling on about my country, but you understand how very important this is to me. How important it is to Africa."

"I think we've had this conversation before, General," O'Neal told him. "We all think this is worthwhile or we wouldn't be here. Right now, I'd like to know about the arms shipments the CIA smuggled into your country."

"Comment?" Zabibu stared at O'Neal with astonishment.

"How did you learn of this, *mon capitaine*?"

"A patron saint told me," O'Neal replied gruffly. "Now, what kind of arms are they?"

"American-manufactured," Zabibu began. "Surplus military weapons. Colt Nineteen-eleven A-one semiautomatic pistols, I believe. Also Smith & Wesson thirty-eight Specials, M-Sixteen assault rifles, M-Seventy-nine grenade launchers. Also, of course, ammunition for all the weapons."

"You won't be fighting any wars with an arsenal of small arms like that," Fanelli commented, lighting a cigarette and shaking his head. "The Company isn't exactly building up your national defenses."

"Wars can be fought with arrows, spears, and even rocks," Caine corrected. The former Katu warrior smiled and added, "Or so I've heard."

"The CIA has made some screw-ups in the past," O'Neal commented, "but I don't think this is one of 'em. The Company couldn't very well supply Kilembe with jets and missile silos."

"We'll have to take inventory of the weapons," Wentworth remarked. He turned to Zabibu. "How bad are the terrorist attacks?"

"Getting worse," the general answered. "As you know, the terrorists have been attacking civilians—farming villages and fishng hamlets along the river. Peasants who are unarmed and unskilled at fighting. So we sent soldiers to protect them, but the terrorists are too great in number and too well armed. Many of our soldiers have been killed. The Kilemban military isn't very large to begin with, and I'm afraid the enemy is gradually whittling it down."

"How dedicated are the people to making this new republic work?" O'Neal asked, helping himself to the glass of brandy both Fanelli and Caine had previously refused. "I don't mean how dedicated are you and the rest of the leaders of the Kilemban government. Are the people really as supportive of this new country as you've said they are?"

"Of course," Zabibu replied, clearly offended by the question. "This is not a dictatorship. The people are not forced to stay in Kilembe against their will."

"Jacob," Wentworth said gently. "Don't get upset, but the fact is many African peasants understand absolutely nothing about politics. They've never known a free government that allowed them to vote or have any say in their government. How dedicated can they be to democracy when they can barely grasp the concept?"

"A man doesn't need a formal education to wish to be free," Zabibu insisted. "You don't know the African people well enough to judge them."

"People are pretty much the same everywhere in the world," O'Neal told him, sipping the brandy. The second glass didn't taste any better than the first. He wondered how much a guy had to drink before this shit improved. "In Vietnam we saw a lot of people who were victims from every side of the war. They didn't feel any great loyalty toward the South Vietnamese government and they were scared shitless of the NVA and the Vietcong. They damn sure didn't trust us or any of the other foreigners involved in the conflict. What they believed in was survival. They wanted to stay alive and they wanted to protect their families and friends in the village. What the hell were they supposed to believe in? Politics is pretty obscure to people who are more concerned about feeding their kids and trying not to get a bullet from any of the soldiers who claimed to be on their side."

"The Angolans who have become Kilembans believe in what we're doing as much as former Zaïrois such as myself," Zabibu stated. "That's why parts of both countries are now Kilembe. Perhaps they don't fully understand democracy, but they know what they've left. Many remember when they lived under the rule of the Belgians or the Portuguese. When they were second-class citizens in their own countries. That's why they're here. All of us want something better for ourselves, for our children, and for the future of all of Africa.''

"That's great," O'Neal said without enthusiasm. "But you're kidding yourself if you don't think a lot of Kilembans are going to collaborate with the enemy when the going gets rough. They'll figure that's the best way to save themselves and protect their families. I'm not puttin' them down for that either, because so far it looks like they're right.''

"They're right?" The general glared at O'Neal.

"Your military can't protect them," the Hard Corps leader explained. "They aren't able to protect themselves because you say they're unarmed and untrained. You said your constitution is modeled after that of the United States, right? You got something in there like the Second Amendment, which gives folks the right to keep and bear arms?''

"We've been debating that issue . . ." Zabibu said lamely.

"Settle it and arm your people," O'Neal insisted. "You can't have soldiers everywhere. That means you need a civilian militia that's armed and trained to defend itself. Why the hell do you think the terrorists have found your people to be such easy targets?''

"Any idea where the terrorists are coming from?" Wentworth asked. "Are they strictly outsiders or are some Kilembe individuals involved?''

"The terrorists have not been identified and they haven't officially declared to be members of any political faction or nationality," Zabibu answered. "However, most of the incidents have occurred near the Angolan border. I don't think any of our own people are participating in these terrible actions—at least not directly. I'll allow the possibility that some may be giving shelter to the enemy out of fear for their lives and the lives of their families.''

"So most of the terrorists are probably coming from Angola," O'Neal mused. "That's what we figured. Lots of Russians and Cubans in Angola. We think either or both of 'em were responsible for that attempt on your life in New York, General.''

"The Soviets do have a lot of influence in Africa," Wentworth added. "They practically own Ethiopia, for instance."

"Slight exaggeration," Zabibu replied. "But only slight. You must understand that Communism has been gaining more ground in Africa because so many of the forms of government here are corrupt and unpopular."

"Okay," O'Neal began, less interested in African politics in general than the situation they were currently faced with. "So we know the Angolans are sending in terrorists. What about Zaire?"

"No," Zabibu assured him. "The government of Zaire isn't any happier about Kilembe than the Angolans, but I'm sure Zaire would never send terrorists or carry out any sort of organized violence against our nation. The fact that Kilembe is a democracy would deter Zaire from such action. Zaire doesn't want to jeopardize relations with the West."

"But they closed the border," O'Neal reminded him.

"I know," Zabibu said with a nod. "Zaire is cutting off all trade and transportation between our two countries. They're hoping we'll fall apart economically. If Kilembe is unable to stand on its own, our government will fall, the country will dissolve, and all territories will go back to the original owners—Zaire and Angola."

"The situation is like Biafra revisited," O'Neal said with a sigh. "You sure you people know what you're in for?"

"You must have realized this would be difficult, Captain," Zabibu replied.

"Difficult?" O'Neal shook his head. "It's damn near impossible. Still, we'll see what we can do."

"We appreciate this, Captain," Zabibu stated. "Whatever the fate of the Republic of Kilembe, we will always be grateful for your help. Money alone isn't an adequate way to show this."

"Just don't forget to pay us," O'Neal replied. "Now, I think we'd better get some sleep and start work in the morning."

"Of course," Zabibu agreed as he moved behind his desk and opened a drawer. "But first, I have something for you."

The general placed four packets on his desk. He opened one and removed two silver eagle insignia. Zabibu handed them to William O'Neal.

"Congratulations," he declared. "You now have the honorary rank of full colonel for as long as you are attached to the armed forces of the Kilemban Republic as a military instructor and special observer."

"Sure never thought I'd ever be.a colonel," O'Neal said with a smile. "Thank you, sir."

"James Wentworth," Zabibu began, opening another packet. "You are now an honorary lieutenant colonel."

"Thank you, sir," Wentworth replied, clicking his heels together as he stood rigidly at attention and saluted the general.

"West Point suck-ass," Fanelli muttered under his breath.

"What was that, Sergeant?" Wentworth demanded.

"Huh?" Fanelli replied lamely. "Oh, I was just thinkin' out loud."

"You were thinking?" Wentworth asked, clipping the silver oak-leaf insignia to his collar as he gazed suspiciously at Fanelli. "Something new for you, Sergeant?"

"He's not a sergeant any longer," Zabibu announced as he handed two gold oak leaves to Fanelli. "Congratulations, Major."

"Major?" Wentworth stared at Fanelli and Zabibu as if both men had suddenly burst into flames. "You're giving *him* a field-grade rank as a commissioned officer?"

"Hot damn," Fanelli grinned. "Guess that means we'll be hanging out at the officers' club now. Huh, Lieu— Colonel?"

"Jacob," Wentworth began. "This man was never an officer and I feel—"

"Let it rest, Jim," O'Neal told him. "These are honorary ranks. Doesn't really mean anything except it gives us all enough clout to order the other soldiers around. Don't worry about it."

"But, *Major* Fanelli?" Wentworth's face contorted into a pained expression as if he might be ill.

"I don't see what the problem is," Zabibu remarked.

"There isn't any problem," Wentworth assured him, trying to avoid looking at Fanelli's grinning face.

"Very well." Zabibu turned to Caine. "I'm afraid we haven't been formally introduced, so I don't know your name."

"Does it really matter, sir?" Caine asked simply.

"Well, I am promoting you to honorary major," the general stated as he handed the insigniae to Caine.

"Okay," the bearded mercenary replied, calmly accepting the new rank.

"Will that be all, General?" O'Neal asked.

"One more thing," Zabibu answered, again moving behind his desk. "I have something special for Colonel Wentworth. You used to be quite a swordsman when I knew you back at Fort Benjamin Harrison. Japanese fencing. What is that called? *Kendo*?"

"My style is *kenjutsu*," Wentworth answered. "It is a more aggressive form of sword-fighting than *kendo*."

"Then I'm sure you'll know more about this than I do," Zabibu stated as he removed a long Japanese sword from under his desk.

Wentworth smiled as Zabibu handed him the sword. The long handle was wrapped in twisted black silk and sharkskin. The round handguard was made of copper and the long blade was encased in a battered brown wood scabbard.

"This seems to be a World War II officer's *katana*," Wentworth stated as he eased the blade from its scabbard. He examined the high-quality steel and razor edge. "Factory-made, of course, and not as valuable or durable as the handmade *katana* swords of the samurai. A very fine sword, though. Where did you find it?"

"I purchased it from a collector six months ago," Zabibu explained. "I don't really know where he got it. The fellow was an Asian of some sort and had trade connections with Hong Kong exporters. When I saw the sword, I thought of you, James. In a sense, this sword inspired me to contact you again."

"Six months ago," Wentworth mused. "That was before you'd even formed the Republic of Kilembe."

"True," the general confirmed. "But even then, I knew we'd have trouble from the other countries. I suspected we might need to get outside help and considered the possibility of hiring mercenaries. I figured that would be the line of work you'd wind up in eventually. You just aren't cut out for classrooms and drill and ceremony, *mon ami*. A peacetime army would bore you to death. War isn't hell for you. Stagnation is."

"I won't deny any of that," Wentworth replied. "Thank you for this wonderful gift."

"You're very welcome," Zabibu said with a nod. "Now, I'd better let you men get some rest. Enjoy it while you can. You'll find very little stagnation while you're here."

"Thank God," Fanelli commented without enthusiasm.

CHAPTER 8

THE REPUBLIC OF Kilembe lay south of the Kaszi River, in a bulging pocket of Southwestern Zaire, stretching on down the Cuango toward Saurino in Angola. It didn't look like much on the map, not that many maps included the tiny fledgling nation.

The main army base, outside the capital city of Kilembe, had looked better in the dead of night. Kilemban soldiers seemed to spend most of their time lounging about the wooden barracks. Many played dominoes or dice games. Others were sleeping off hangovers. *Radi-pombe*, a crudely processed form of beer with an unusually high alcohol content, seemed very popular with the troops. Some were even drinking bottles of the sudsy brown liquid when the Hard Corps inspected the billets shortly after dawn the following morning. One of the guys on sentry duty had a bottle before O'Neal took it away from him and poured the contents on the ground.

"Jesus," O'Neal muttered as he examined the undisciplined and neglected condition of the billets. "This is gonna be harder than I thought."

"Jacob admitted discipline was poor," Wentworth reminded the Hard Corps commander. "He hasn't had time to supervise the troops personally, and most of his best officers and noncoms are in the field with the more experienced troops patrolling the region for terrorists."

"Shit," Fanelli snorted. "I've seen teenage street gangs that were better disciplined than this bunch."

"So let's get to work on 'em," O'Neal suggested. He turned his attention to the troops. "On your feet and stand at attention by your bunks!"

Wentworth translated the order and repeated it in loud French. Many soldiers didn't understand either language, but other troopers explained the order. About half the men gradually obeyed the command. Many were still asleep and a few continued to roll dice and bet on the outcome, choosing to ignore the white men.

"I see we need some drastic methods here," O'Neal growled as he drew a .45 Colt pistol from the holster on his hip.

He thumbed off the safety catch and aimed the pistol at a case of beer bottles at the end of the bay area. He picked an easy target because he was still unfamiliar with this particular side arm from the CIA arms shipment. O'Neal fired a single 230-grain hard-ball slug into the case. Wood splintered and glass shattered. The roar of the big-bore pistol thundered in the confined area.

Men cried out in alarm and fear. A few grabbed weapons. One even pointed his French MAT-49 submachine gun at O'Neal. Steve Caine silently slipped past a row of bunks and aimed his .45 at the gunman's head. The guy dropped his weapon and stepped into the center of the room. Everybody was awake now and paying attention. Someone cursed in Lingala as a pool of brown liquid appeared at the base of the beer case.

"Good morning, gentlemen," O'Neal declared. "Now, get outside and in formation . . . shit. Jim, Joe, get 'em in something that looks a little like a formation."

"We'll try," Wentworth replied. *"Sortez de la caserne! Comprenez-vous? Vite! Vite!"*

They herded the troops from the billets and eventually got them standing in rows in front of the building. Wentworth remained with the troops and made certain none wandered off or carried weapons. The others rounded up soldiers from other billets, until they had the bulk of the base personnel standing in the parade field.

"All right," O'Neal began as he addressed the men. He guessed there were about four hundred soldiers present. He didn't even want to think where the others might be. "I'm Colonel O'Neal. You'll get to know who the rest of these officers are because we're going to make some changes in your lifestyle. First change is, you're going to start acting like soldiers. So stand up straight, damn it! Show some pride for yourselves and the profession you're in. The rest of your countrymen are depending on you to protect them. If you expect to earn their respect, you should start by showing some respect for yourselves."

Wentworth translated O'Neal's speech and other soldiers converted the words into other languages until all present understood. More than half the troopers began to straighten their backs and raise their chins. The pep talk was already achieving some desired effects. But other soldiers still appeared unimpressed.

"Colonel," a soldier began in broken English, "we no have to take from you any orders. We are democracy now. Everybody equal now."

"You're in the army and an army is never a democracy, fella," O'Neal replied. *"No democracy.* Got that? And keep your mouth shut in my formation unless I give you permission to speak. Nobody ever understands shit if everybody's talking at the same time. Right now, you shut up and listen."

The man glared at O'Neal, but he didn't utter a reply.

"This guy here mentioned a democracy," O'Neal stated. "Maybe you figure that means everybody can do whatever they want. Sorry, but it doesn't work that way. What it means is your people now have the freedom to make decisions. The right to participate in their government, in the laws, and the right to choose what goals you want in life and go after them. But all that good stuff has a price. You see, you got a whole bunch of new responsibilities. If you don't get involved or put in any effort and just don't give a damn, then your democracy will either be corrupted, or outsiders will come in and take it away from you. You've all lived under other forms of government so I don't have to tell you what they're like."

The translations took a while and O'Neal allowed enough time for the message to sink in before he continued.

"While you're in the army you have a responsibility to protect your country," O'Neal stated. "That means you're going to have to follow orders so you can learn how to work as a fighting unit and successfully combat opponents who have been trained and disciplined to fight as a team. To teach you how to work together, we're going to have you do a lot of stuff that will seem like bullshit. You'll have to march together, clean up messes together—starting with that pigsty you call a barracks—stand in dumbass formations and dress alike. I want you all to wear something that looks more like a uniform from now on."

O'Neal waited for translations to finish before he spoke again.

"Okay," O'Neal continued, pacing slowly in front of the ragtag collection of troops. Expressions on their dark faces ranged from fear to eagerness, with anger, disinterest, and boredom among the other expressions. "I don't know where the rest of your company is right now. Some are on patrol, but I figure the rest are still at home with the wife and kids. A lot of others are probably in a town or village where they spent the night gettin' drunk or gettin' laid, or both—if they were lucky. That sort of behavior comes to a halt right now. We got a war going on, damn it. Nobody leaves this base without permission. You wanna go someplace and spend the night with a woman or a bottle? You goddamn earn it first. When your buddies come back, they'll get this same lecture.''

O'Neal folded his arms on his chest and glared into the face of one of the angry troopers. The man met his stare for a moment and looked away.

"Now, understand this and listen real careful 'cause I damn well mean it," O'Neal declared. ''Anyone who goes AWOL—absent without leave—his action will be regarded as desertion. Since we got a war going on, deserters will be regarded as traitors and that is a court-martial offense, which can be punished by death. In short, run out on me and I'll kill you. One of you guys pointed a gun at me earlier. Since your training and discipline hasn't been worth a shit, I'll let that incident slide *this* time. Anybody who aims a gun at any officer, noncom, or fellow soldier in this army will find himself facing charges of attempted murder and conspiracy to sabotage the foundations of this military service, and thus attempting conspiracy against the Kilemban government itself. That's a capital offense. I will personally put a bullet in your head if you pull a stunt like that.''

The silence among the troops was absolute. O'Neal let them think about what he'd said before he added his final comments.

"I want all officers and NCOs to fall out," O'Neal announced. "I want to talk to them in private. The rest of you guys will start cleaning up the barracks. You got two hours to get the place looking decent. Then you'll have some physical training and whatever else before lunch. What are we eating for lunch, anyway?''

"I checked out the mess hall," Fanelli answered. "Not quite sure what the food is. Looked like leaves, bamboo shoots, fish, and stale bread.''

"Fuck that!" O'Neal said sharply. "By twelve hundred hours I want at least four cows or buffalo or whatever to be slaughtered and cooked for lunch. My men are gonna damn well have decent food to look forward to after a hard day of training.''

A collective cheer erupted from the ranks. Of course, that was exactly the reaction O'Neal had hoped for. He dismissed the men to see to their "GI party" in the barracks and gathered the officers and noncoms in a group. Wentworth stayed with him to translate while Caine and Fanelli supervised the men.

"I didn't want to chew you guys out in front of the troops," O'Neal told the junior officers and noncoms. "So I'll do it now. I've never seen such a fucked-up excuse for a military base in my life—and I've seen some pretty big fuck-ups in the past. You expect these men to become soldiers just because you give them a gun and a uniform? Bullshit.''

"We did the best we could," a young lieutenant stated. He shrugged and held his hands out with open palms. "We have been given ignorant baboons. What do you expect?''

The lieutenant, O'Neal realized, was educated, and he had developed a prejudice toward those Africans he considered to be backward. "I don't want to hear that sort of talk," O'Neal told him. "If you can't keep your prejudice to yourself and treat these men like human beings and teach them to be soldiers, I'll kick your ass out of this military outfit. That goes for the rest of you as well.''

"I haven't been able to find any sort of training schedule around here," Wentworth announced. "We can't be sure if the troops have received any training in weapons, tactics, hygiene, or anything else.''

"We're low on ammunition," a young captain explained. "We can't afford to waste it with target practice—"

"Then we'll have them dry-fire," O'Neal declared.

"We'll take them to a firing range. Have them treat empty weapons as if they're loaded at all times. Then we'll teach them firearm safety, maintenance, how to aim and fire the weapons. That's the most important part of basic instruction in shooting anyway. After everybody knows how to handle his weapon, we'll let them fire a few rounds just to get accustomed to the recoil and pull of the barrel when the gun is fired."

"Meantime," Wentworth added, "I suggest we get all weapons away from the troops until they've been instructed in the use of the firearms. Guns in the hands of the ignorant are how accidents occur. Presently, they're more of a threat to each other than to the terrorists."

"I agree," O'Neal stated. "Now, how long has it been since the soldiers were paid?"

"Paid?" The captain seemed surprised. "They haven't been paid. They receive food, clothing, and shelter. Since they are serving their country to defend it from aggression, I don't see why they should expect payment."

"Because soldiers are human and they like to have money in their pockets," O'Neal insisted. "You can't expect men to be patriotic when they can't see that they're getting any sort of personal benefit from the system they're protecting. We'll have to arrange some way to pay the troops. I want this taken care of by the end of the week. These guys are gonna be pissed off after they've gone through some real training and getting paid at the end of the week will boost morale. Don't kid yourselves, gentlemen. Our soldiers might mutiny if we don't treat them right. It's happened before when troops were neglected or got too much stick and not enough carrot."

He examined the NCOs. All of the noncoms were big men, heavyset and well muscled. O'Neal guessed how they'd gotten promoted to NCO rank.

"That goes for excessive bully-boy tactics, too," O'Neal warned. "I don't want leaders who rely on muscles to intimidate the men. Muscles don't mean shit against a bullet. I want intelligent leaders who can think for themselves and instruct men without having to resort to beatings. You mistreat the troops and they'll come to regard you as the enemy, not the terrorists.''

"Anything else, Colonel?" the disgruntled lieutenant asked with a sniff.

"Quite a bit," O'Neal replied. "Among other things, I want the names of all the troops who have wives or family within immediate distance of the base. I want them to be able to spend a reasonable amount of time with their families. Also, I want to know where the closest whorehouse is located."

"I don't know of any whorehoues in Kilembe," the captain declared with astonishment.

"What kind of soldier are you, man?" O'Neal replied gruffly. "Look, we've got a bunch of young men here. Young men get horny and wanna get laid. Get—laid. Understand? I want them to be able to go some place we know about to get their jollies. If there isn't a whorehouse around, we'll see about building one. Gotta be some local talent around here for that sort of business."

"I find your advice questionable," the lieutenant stated.

"I don't give a shit," O'Neal told him. "We've got a job to do and, like it or not, we're doing it our way."

CHAPTER 9

THE TERRORISTS APPROACHED their target. Eduardo Winchi led the attack force of twenty-seven well-armed Angolan shock troops. All were experienced in hit-and-run terrorist tactics, but none of the lesser-ranking members of the team could match Winchi's first-hand knowledge of guerrilla warfare.

An Ovimbundu, Winchi despised his Portuguese first name and regarded it as a burden placed upon him by his gutless parents who, in his opinion, had been boot-licking lackies of the European colonialists who'd oppressed his people for five centuries. Eduardo Winchi was only ten years old when he ran away from home to join the Marxist revolutionary forces in 1972.

Indeed, the history of Portuguese rule in Angola had not been pleasant. About one million Africans had been shipped out of Angolan ports as slaves bound for Portuguese colonies in Brazil. Opposition to Portuguese control of Angola had

increased as the hope of driving out the European rulers
finally seemed possible in the twentieth century. Many other
African nations had already gained independence. In fact,
Angola was the last major European colony to achieve this
goal. Finally, in 1975, the Portuguese relinquished their
hold on Angola.

However, civil war erupted between the rival political
factions. The Marxist-led Popular Movement for the Liber-
ation of Angola received assistance from the Soviet Union
and thousands of troops from Cuba. In 1976 the MPLA
emerged as the victorious political group. Fourteen-year-old
Eduardo Winchi was among the MPLA heroes of the revolution.

Winchi had fought on many battlefields since then. He
had joined Cuban forces in the civil war against Jonas
Savimbi and his Union for the Total Independence of Angola, or UNITA, which still controls a large portion of the
southern part of the country. In June 1980 he had fought
invading South African troops. Only twenty-seven years
old, Eduardo Winchi had spent almost two-thirds of his life
as a Marxist revolutionary and guerrilla fighter.

But the constant years of strife and hardship had taken
their toll, and Winchi had recently lost control of his original
vision. He had become more uncompromising, more brutal.
A small group of UNITA prisoners his men had captured
recently were personally, ritualistically executed by him.
After Kilembe declared independence, Winchi became even
more driven. He wanted to wipe the new country out, exter-
minate those who were responsible for infringing on his
homeland's territory.

The terrorist band arrived at the edge of the jungle. Winchi
gestured for his men to stay back and remain silent. Stealth-
ily, the MPLA veteran crawled on his belly with an AK-47
assault rifle braced across his bent elbows. He slithered
through the elephant grass and carefully raised his head to
scan the area of the small farming village.

Winchi curled his lip with disgust. The design of the houses, with wooden walls bonded together with adobe clay and hutlike roofing of oil palm branches reinforced by tar, suggested the villagers belonged to the Bakongo. Winchi had always considered the Bakongo to be inferior to the Ovimbundu, although the languages and customs of the two peoples were similar in many ways.

The farmers and their families were busy working in fields of tall cornstalks. Corn is a major agricultural crop in Angola and Winchi considered the southern portion of Kilembe to still be part of Angola. The Bakongo farmers were traitors and cowards who'd gone along with the political blasphemy of the new independent republic. Winchi and his team intended to make them pay dearly for this heresy.

Scouts had been sent ahead of the attack force to check the village for signs of Kilemban military patrols. They had found no evidence of any soldiers: nothing but seventy or eighty Bakongo peasants hard at work. Women were busy grinding corn into meal for bread. Men, clad in cotton shorts and hats of woven reeds, chopped down stalks and gathered fresh ears of corn.

Winchi rose to his feet and carefully canted his Kalashnikov rifle across a shoulder. He gestured for the others to come forward. The terrorists emerged from the brush, Soviet-made weapons held ready.

"*Askari!*" a woman cried, pointing at the terrorists. "*Pale askari!*"

The women ran to their houses. Winchi and his men raised their rifles and aimed at the male workers, but the farmers had suddenly disappeared among the cornstalks. The terrorists swung their weapons toward the women only to discover that they, too, had vanished. Winchi immediately sensed something was wrong, but he couldn't put a finger on what it was.

Suddenly, automatic-rifle fire erupted. Winchi threw himself to the ground as high-velocity bullets hissed above his trembling form. He heard the voices of two of his men cry out in pain, followed by the rustle of grass and thuds as bodies hit the ground. A wounded terrorist groaned and rolled about, clutching a trio of bullet holes between his breastbone and navel. Two other Angolan hitmen were already dead. One had been shot through the heart and the other had been taken out by a classic right-between-the-eyes bull's-eye.

"*Automatico espingardas!*" one of the terrorists cried, stating in Portuguese what was already all to obvious.

"*Quieto!*" Winchi snapped as he hugged the ground and pointed his AK-47 in the general direction of the sniper fire. "Keep your heads down and your mouths shut!"

He couldn't figure where the shots had come from. It had all happened too fast, too unexpectedly. Winchi suddenly realized what had been wrong about the village. He had seen no children working or playing outside the huts. The farmers and their women had responded to the terrorists in an organized, well-rehearsed manner—as if they had been drilled in how to handle such a situation.

James Wentworth crouched at the doorway of the house of the village chief. A whisp of smoke rose from the barrel of his M-16 assault rifle. Wentworth grunted with satisfaction at his marksmanship with a weapon he hadn't had a chance to zero-in on a firing range. He'd fired only one shot and nailed his target in the head.

Joe Fanelli and the three Kilemban soldiers with him had made the other two hits. So far the mercenaries' defense plan had worked as perfectly as a Swiss timepiece, but even a clock made by Swiss experts can fuck up, and the mercs knew it.

"*Puis-je adier?*" the village chief asked as he sat on the floor of the hut with a rusty old WWII Mauser rifle across his folded legs.

The rest of the peasants were relatively safe, either hidden

in basement storage compartments or crouched behind a
row of sandbags in the cornfield. The chief had insisted on
staying with the defenders to help if possible. He was probably more than seventy and he didn't have any ammunition
for his rifle—Wentworth doubted the mistreated old gun
would fire anyway—but the old guy had guts.

"Merci beaucoup," Wentworth told the chief. "Right
now, the best way you can help is to stay down so I don't
have to make certain you're not in the line of fire. As I
burn up ammunition and toss the empty magazines, you
could reload them for me, *s'il vous plaît."*

A volley of automatic fire snarled outside. Fanelli and
the three Kilemban soldiers were keeping the enemy pinned
down with a steady stream of bullets. Another terrorist
screamed as slugs punched through his ribs and chest.

Fanelli was posted at the rear of another house. He lowered
his rifle and leaned it against the wall, before gathering up
an M-79 grenade launcher and a walkie-talkie. He braced
the stock of the launcher against a hip and switched on the
two-way radio.

"Hey, Colonel," he spoke into the device. "This is *Major*
Fanelli. Talk to your fellow field-grade officer, sweetheart."

"Cut the crap," Wentworth's voice ordered in reply.
"How's the situation look from your angle?"

"We took a few guys out, but there's still about twenty
of the bastards left to deal with. I'm ready to flush 'em out,
Colonel."

"Do it," Wentworth replied gruffly. "We'll be ready."

"You got it," Fanelli said, and promptly put down the
radio to handle the M-79 with both hands.

He aimed the short-barreled launcher at the elephant grass
where the terrorists were hidden. Fanelli squeezed the trigger
and fired a 40-mm grenade into the enemies' position. The
projectile exploded with a burst of light and flame. The
blast ripped three terrorists to shreds and hurled their mangled corpses into the sky. The force of the explosion reached

Winchi and two other Angolans. They were thrown several feet by the impact. Winchi lost his grip on his AK-47 and fell to earth in a daze. One of his pals slammed headfirst into the trunk of an African cedar. His skull cracked open like an eggshell and left an ugly stain of blood and brain tissue on the tree.

Surviving terrorists bolted in all directions. Several dashed back into the jungle. Two were stupid enough to run straight for the village. Wentworth was ready for them, the selector switch of his M-16 set on full auto. The mercenary squeezed off two well-controlled three-round bursts. Each terrorist received a welcoming trio of 5.56-mm slugs in the chest, left of center. The targets went down with their hearts ripped apart.

Other opponents ran to the east of the village, trying to get into a better position to fire at the defenders. The three Kilemban troopers saw the group break cover and began shooting their M-16 rifles. They were inexperienced soldiers, but the Hard Corps had trained them well since the mercenaries had arrived in Kilembe two weeks before. The trio fired their rifles with quick precision and brought down half a dozen of the enemy.

Their marksmanship was less than exceptional. Bullets tore into the terrorists' chests and abdomens. The Hard Corps had told them to shoot at the easiest target—namely, an opponent's torso. A couple of lucky terrorists died quickly, but most collapsed with bullets buried deep in their stomachs and intestines.

The surviving MPLA guerrillas returned fire. One Kilemban soldier didn't duck for cover fast enough: four 7.62-mm Kalashnikov rounds smashed into his chest and face. He fell lifeless near his two companions as they triggered their M-16s. Meanwhile, another Angolan invader was taken out by several bullets in the upper torso. Two others dropped to kneeling positions and continued to fire at the Kilembans.

Fanelli had swapped his M-79 launcher for his assault

rifle. He saw his men were in trouble and immediately came
to their aid. The Hard Corps merc snap-aimed his M-16 and
fired a quick trio of rounds into the closest opponent. Bullets
smashed into the side of the Angolan's skull and spattered
his brains out a gory exit on the opposite side of his head.

The other terrorist gunman turned his AK-47 toward
Fanelli's position, but the mercenary already had the bastard
in his sights. Fanelli pumped three 5.56-mm high-velocity
slugs into the terrorist's upper chest and throat. The
Kalashnikov fell from the man's quivering fingers as he
dropped backward and convulsed briefly on the ground before his body accepted the final serenity of death.

Four Angolan gunmen headed west, toward the cornfield.
Steve Caine watched them from a camouflaged position at
the edge of the jungle. During the chaos and confusion,
Caine had crept from his original hiding place among the
cornstalks to conceal himself in the brush closer to the
enemies' locale. The mercenary had unscrewed the cap from
the butt of the survival knife handle and removed the fishing
line and a fish hook and hung it on the branch of a *namna-ya-
tunda* bush before creeping silently to a tree trunk ten feet
away.

Caine allowed the terrorists to pass his position before
he swung his M-16 around the edge of the tree and opened
fire. An Angolian hitman screamed as three bullets struck
him between the shoulder blades and snapped his spine like
a dry twig. The others turned and saw their comrade fall.
They raised their weapons and searched the jungle for the
concealed rifleman.

Caine pulled the fishing line. The bush shook and rustled
loudly in response. The terrorists opened fire at the movement. A dozen 7.62-mm slugs tore into the harmless bush
as Steve Caine crouched by the tree trunk away from the
line of fire.

He aimed carefully and shot another terrorist in the side
of the head before the Angolans realized they'd been tricked.

Bullets drilled the man just above the right temple and blasted away the top of his skull. Brains splashed a startled terrorist who turned to see his companion fall. Caine fired again and blasted the man's face apart while it was still wearing an expression of astonishment.

The fourth and final guerrilla swung his Kalashnikov at Caine's position and opened fire. Bullets chipped bark from the tree trunk as Caine dropped into a prone position and returned fire. The gunman cried out and staggered backward with blood seeping from bullet holes in his belly. Caine clucked his tongue with disgust at his own marksmanship and finished off his opponent with a head shot.

Eduardo Winchi and another terrorist gazed up at the two white men who approached him from the village. The rest of the terrorist unit had either been killed or managed to flee back into the jungle. Winchi slowly rose and glared at the figure who stood before him. The white man was dressed in a jungle camouflage uniform and held an M-16 rifle in his fists. He also wore a pistol belt with a side-arm on his right hip and a long sword at the left.

"You want to surrender?" James Wentworth asked. He spoke in English, but his tone was understandable in any language.

Winchi replied by drawing his machete from his belt.

"That's okay, too," Wentworth declared as he tossed his rifle to Fanelli and grabbed the hilt of his sword with his left hand.

He drew the long blade from the scabbard with an overhand grip on the hilt as he stepped forward with his left foot. Winchi raised his machete and charged. Wentworth ducked low and, guiding the blade of the *katana* with his right hand, bolted under the Angolan's jungle knife. The sword slashed a deep cut across Winchi's armpit and shoulder. The terrorist leader shrieked and dropped his machete. Wentworth pivoted and gripped the sword hilt with both hands. He stood behind the wounded man with his *katana* poised in an overhead stance.

Wentworth swung the sword. The second stroke cut a deep diagonal wound through Winchi's neck, slicing arteries and severing vertebrae. The terrorist boss fell to the ground, blood spurting from his slashed neck. Wentworth snapped his wrist to flick blood from the blade of his sword.

"How about you?" Wentworth asked the last member of the terrorist outfit, gesturing at the man with the point of his *katana*. "You want to surrender, or you want to go the same route as your friend?"

The Angolan did not understand English, but he had seen what had happened to Winchi and didn't care to face the same fate. He raised his hands in surrender.

CHAPTER 10

"TOO BAD YOU missed our first engagement with the enemy, Bill," James Wentworth remarked. "One of our men was killed, but considering the fact the attack force was larger than we'd expected, that's not really too bad."

"I imagine the dead man would disagree," William O'Neal replied dryly as he examined one of the Kalashnikov rifles that had been confiscated from the slain terrorists. "Were they all armed with these?"

"A couple were armed with Soviet PPS submachine guns," Wentworth answered, taking the *katana* sword from his belt to sit in a chair by the desk in O'Neal's temporary office at Kilemban military headquarters. "No light machine guns or rocket launchers, and none of the terrorists carried any grenades. At least, none of the men we killed, or the single terrorist we captured. Can't say for certain about those who managed to escape."

"They probably didn't figure they'd need any more weapons than the AKs," O'Neal commented. "After all, they thought they'd only be going up against some peasant farmers. The survivors will certainly report what happened when they get back to Angola. We can't count on future victories being so easy after the enemy learns what happened at that village."

"By the way," Wentworth offered with a broad smile, "congratulations on guessing where the terrorists would strike."

"Well, we knew most of the attacks had been against peasants near the Angolan border," O'Neal replied. "I figured the strategy had worked well for them in the past, so they'd keep using it. Also, I had some of the more experienced veterans of the military patrols shifted to other villages in the area. Figured you guys wouldn't need as much manpower and I wanted some of our greener troops to get a taste of combat. I want these people to know the enemy isn't invincible."

"No one is," Wentworth commented. "How's the training been going while we were gone?"

"Pretty good," O'Neal said with a nod. "We've got some bright, enthusiastic fellows in this little army. They're learning fast and some are beginning to teach others. One problem is the language barrier. You gotta have somebody translate English into French, French into Swahili, and Swahili into God knows what else. Still, that part is coming along remarkably well."

"What parts aren't?" Wentworth asked.

"We don't have enough weapons, radio equipment for communications, or medical supplies for wounded personnel," O'Neal answered in exasperation. "Not enough of anything."

He placed the AK-47 on his desk and stared down at it. "On the other hand," O'Neal added, "the enemy has plenty of these. The Soviets have been supplying weapons and other military necessities to Angolan forces for more than a decade. The Cubans have been there almost as long. You can bet your ass that the Luanda government's cooperating in every way possible with Havana to try to crush Kilembe."

"I didn't think there was any doubt about that," Wentworth remarked. "So what do we do about it?"

"We make the most of what we've got," O'Neal replied, patting the steel frame of the Kalashnikov rifle. "And we get more of these."

"How do you intend to get more guns when all trade into Kilembe has been cut off?" Wentworth asked. He suddenly smiled as he realized what O'Neal meant. "Oh, I understand now. We get the guns the same way we got this one."

"From the enemy," O'Neal confirmed. "Meantime, we need to continue training the defense forces with what weapons we have available."

"The armory isn't exactly overstocked," the Hard Corps XO stated. "The arms vary, too. Belgian and French rifles— many of these being World War II relics. The French arms merchants smuggled in some NATO R-One rifles and the Israelis slipped in some Galil rifles before Zaire closed the border. Of course, we've also got the CIA care package, consisting of less than two hundred arms."

"I know," O'Neal assured him. "We've got weapons that use seven-point-sixty-two, five-point-fifty-six, and nine-millimeter ammo. We've got obsolete rifles in eight millimeter, seven-point-nine mill Belgian Mausers, and handguns in several different calibers. Presents some problems for our troops because the ammuntion they'll be carrying won't be consistent."

"Well, I'd hate to run out of ammo for my M-Sixteen and crawl over to my buddy and find out he was armed with an eight-millimeter rifle," Wentworth commented. "Unless, of course, he happened to be carrying some five-point-fifty-six rounds."

"The way we're handling that is to issue the same type weapons to each separate division of troops," O'Neal explained. "One battalion gets NATO FAL rifles or other seven-point-sixty-two-mill weapons. Another gets M-Sixteens or Galils or whatever in five-point-fifty-six mill. When we get enough Russian weapons to arm a battalion, we'll handle it the same way. Handguns go to officers and a few NCOs."

"What about the weird stuff in eight and seven-point-nine millimeter?" Wentworth asked. "No military in the world uses those calibers anymore."

"Wrong," O'Neal told him. "The Kilemban army uses them. Those are large caliber weapons with a long range. So we'll issue them to the fellows who appear to have the most promise as snipers."

"There still aren't enough weapons to go around," the other merc remarked, "and you want to arm the civilians as well?"

"We'll get more guns," O'Neal promised. "Besides, there are other kinds of weapons. Let's get Joe and Steve. I want you fellows to meet somebody who's going to help us."

"Someone special?" Wentworth inquired, eyebrows raised.

"*Very* special," the Hard Corps commander assured him as he headed for the exit. "You've never met anybody quite like him before."

The Pygmy was barely three-and-a-half feet tall. His compact frame was thin, with cords of muscles vividly outlined along his shoulders and limbs. His skin was a lighter complexion than that of most Africans of the Congo regions, and his curly black hair was piled on his large head and held in place by a copper ring. He was clad only in a loincloth and a necklace. An odd assortment of decorations was attached to the necklace—a piece of wood, a chunk of unpolished ivory, a thick black claw from a lion or leopard, and a small bronze crucifix. Each item was separated from the others by knots in the cord around his neck. The Pygmy didn't want the jewelry to jingle when he moved.

He smiled as the four Hard Corps mercenaries approached. The Pygmy's right hand was fisted around the shaft of a spear while his left held a crudely rolled cigarette. He puffed on the latter item and blew smoke from his nostrils.

O'Neal introduced the Pygmy to Wentworth, Caine, and Fanelli. "This is Chief Moshi, the headman of the local tribe of the Bambute. He knows English and is a great warrior and hunter.

"You call me Moshi, okay?" the Pygmy declared cheerfully. "I speak English good. Learn from missionary person. Also learn of Christian God. Man on cross. You know. Okay?"

"I'm sure the missionary would be pleased," Wentworth said, trying to keep sarcasm from his voice. "A pleasure to meet you, Chief Moshi."

"Just Moshi," the chief insisted. "My tribe want help fight enemies of Kilembe. We hear talk of freedom on radio. We want freedom."

"I believe you, Moshi," Steve Caine said with a nod. His years with the Katu had given him special insight into the attitudes of people whose cultures were very different. "I have heard of the Bambute magic. I'd be interested to see your magic, and show you some magic I have learned in return. Unless this would not please your people. Some magic is not to be shared and some ways are not meant for others to know. I would not wish to offend the ways of your people."

"Most white man laugh and tell us we are wrong," Moshi said with a frown.

"I will not laugh," Caine promised.

"Okay, white man." Moshi smiled. "We teach you a little Bambute magic and you teach us some too. What you got?"

"Warrior magic," Caine replied with a smile.

"That sound good okay," the Pygmy agreed.

"Major Caine will go with you, Chief Moshi," O'Neal told the Pygmy. "He will represent all of us and work with your people. I have absolute faith in his judgment. If you wish, I will accompany you as well, but I will have to return here to help with other matters."

"That's okay," Moshi assured him. "Major be okay with us. You okay look after people without Bambute magic."

"Thank you, Moshi," O'Neal said with a nod. He turned to Caine. "You want to spend a week or so with the Bambute?"

"Absolutely," Caine replied, handing his rifle to Fanelli. "I won't need this. Take care of it until I get back."

"Wait a minute, Tarzan," Fanelli began, reluctant to take his partner's M-16. "You might need this gun, for crissake. Don't forget terrorists are running around this chunk of jungle real estate."

"The Bambute don't have guns and we won't be able to supply them with any—at least not for a long time yet," Caine told him. "I don't want to take a rifle among them when we can't give them such weapons. It wouldn't be right. I've still got a forty-five side arm. That's enough in an emergency that I can't handle with this."

Caine patted the hilt of his survival knife.

"Jesus," Fanelli muttered. "You'd think that damn pig-sticker was a cloak of invisibility or somethin'."

"Don't worry about me, Joe." Caine grinned. "You guys will have enough to handle on your own. If I'm not back in nine days, figure I'm not coming back at all."

"Fair enough, Steve," O'Neal replied. "Take care of yourself, and good luck."

Caine shook hands with each of his partners before he left the military base with Moshi. The three mercs watched Caine and the Pygmy walk from the gates of the compound and eventually disappear from view. The mercs knew Caine and Moshi would continue across the grassy plains to the rain forest beyond.

"Let's get back to work," O'Neal told his men. "Joe, I want you to see what sort of improvised explosives you can come up with. We don't have many grenades or other explosives here. Zabibu promised to get us a couple of chemists who can help you come up with something better than regular stick dynamite."

"Sure," Fanelli answered, still staring in the direction where Caine and Moshi had headed. "Damn it, I wish Steve hadn't gone off by himself like that. Last time he went into a jungle without us we didn't see him again for more than three years."

"He knows what he's doing," Wentworth stated. "Caine will do his job. We have to do ours."

"Yeah," Fanelli agreed, but he couldn't help wondering if they'd ever see Steve Caine again.

CHAPTER 11

LUIS PEREZ EXAMINED a wall map of the continent of Africa. The Cuban G-2 officer jammed a black pin into a section still marked as part of northern Angola although the Republic of Kilembe now claimed it to be part of the new territory. Numerous red pins had previously been stuck in the map. These labeled successful attacks on villages and hamlets within Kilembe by Angolan forces.

The black pin marked a victory for the other side.

The overhead ceiling fan cast a moving shadow across the map, like the flapping black wing of an African wing vulture. Appropriate, Perez mused. The map was a chart of death. The campaign had been one-sided until Winchi's company had been all but wiped out by village defenders.

This defeat nagged at Perez more than the statistics on the map justified. However, Perez had know Eduardo Winchi. The terrorist had been one of the few Angolans whom Perez had regarded as a competent guerrilla fighter. Winchi had been very experienced and he'd commanded an unusually large number of troops to take on a single village. Perez had ordered the larger attack force to insure victory in case a Kilemban patrol arrived during the assault. Twenty-eight men had attacked that tiny little farm village and only three had managed to return to Angola alive.

"Boa tarde, Capitão," João Jangwa saluted as he entered the Cuban's office at the temporary base in the Cuango valley. *"Como esta—"*

"Falar espanhol!" Perez snapped, speaking one of the few expressions in Portuguese he had managed to master during his past service in Angola. "You speak to me in Spanish, Comrade. And I am now *Colonel* Perez, not Captain. *Comprende?"*

"Sí," Jangwa replied with a forced smile. "Congratulations, Comrade Colonel. I'm sure you are happy about your well-deserved promotion. And welcome back to the Republic of Angola."

"I would sooner return to a Cuban pigsty," Perez spat. "You and I are not strangers, Comrade Jangwa. Let's not waste time with social niceties or Party slogans. We don't like each other very much, but we have a common goal. You know why Havana sent me back?"

"Of course," the heavyset Angolan confirmed, folding his muscular arms on his barrel chest. "I just hope you do better against Kilembe than your countrymen have done against Savimbi's rebel forces in southern Angola."

"We will succeed, Jangwa," Perez answered. "You and I and Comrade Baridi are going to work together, and work together *well*. I trust you know of Baridi?"

"Sí," Jangwa said with a nod. "Marcel Baridi. A Bakongo from the People's Republic of the Congo who speaks French, Lingala, and a little Kikongo. I'm grateful that Brazzaville has decided to send in some support, but we've as much trouble understanding him as you have understanding Portuguese. You know that he doesn't speak Spanish?"

"He speaks English," Perez stated. "Don't worry, I can understand Baridi. What I don't understand is why Winchi's company failed to take that village." He pointed at the black pin on the map.

"I've spoken with the survivors, Colonel," Jangwa replied. "They said the villagers were ready for the attack. The peasants, it seems, had help. Men armed with automatic rifles and either a grenade launcher or a rocket launcher. Whoever they were, they were certainly more efficient than the usual patrols."

"No idea who they might be?" Perez asked with a frown.

"Supposedly," Jangwa continued, "at least one of the defenders was a white man. Could be CIA. Or one of those American 'Soldiers of fortune.' "

"Perhaps," the Cuban admitted as he put his hands behind his back and began to pace the floor of the small office. "That renegade Zabibu spent four years in America. He may have received training at the CIA headquarters. Information on Zabibu is rather limited. However, CIA agents aren't generally combat experts. Of course, Zabibu may have made contact with the CIA while in New York recently and he may have been supplied with agents experienced with the old Special Operations Group in Vietnam."

"I thought the Americans didn't want to get involved in the Kilembe affair," Jangwa remarked.

"Neither do the Russians." Perez laughed. "Moscow doesn't want to be involved in this either, but they want the outcome to be in their favor."

"The Russians do not own Angola, Colonel," Jangwa reminded Perez.

"They don't own East Germany, Poland, or Czechoslovakia either," Perez replied. "Or Cuba. That's why I'm here, eh? Because Cuba just wants to help you Angolans because we're so committed to world socialism? You're not stupid, Comrade. None of the idealistic young zealots are present, so let's not pretend that we don't realize that we're all pawns in a great chess game by the Soviets and the Americans. Both Cubans and Angolans are playing on the Soviet side. Kilembe wants to join the American camp. The United States is probably involved in this conflict one way or the other. Washington will certainly be willing to recognize the government of Kilembe at the next General Assembly meeting of the UN although they still refuse to acknowledge the government of Angola.''

''*Yanqui porcos*,'' Jangwa spat, slipping into Portuguese as he cursed the Americans.

''Still,'' the Cuban officer mused, gazing at the map as if seeking divine guidance from the chart, ''as you said, the white men may not be connected with the CIA—at least, not directly. Zabibu may have hired American or European mercenaries to help his little army fight back.''

''Indeed.'' Jangwa recalled the American mercenaries caught and tried in a Luanda kangaroo court a few years back.

Perez went on. ''Jacob Zabibu is old enough to recall when his homeland of Zaire was still the Belgian Congo,'' he explained, putting a thin cheroot in his lips and lighting it with a match. ''After the Belgians gave his country independence, civil war occurred in Zaire between Lumumba''—he referred to Patrice Lumumba, the leftist ruler of independent Zaire—''and Moise Tshombe, a Christian fanatic who dreamed of modeling the new Congo nation into a democracy. No doubt, Zabibu regards himself to be a modern day Tshombe.''

''I've heard this history lesson before,'' Jangwa said with a sigh. ''The noble Lumumba was murdered by imperialist soldiers and the Soviet Union honors that great patriot of the world socialist movement to this very day. The Patrice Lumumba University recognizes his achievements, and would-be revolutionaries from Third World countries travel to the Soviet Union to study at this university named in honor of our great deceased comrade.''

"Muy bien," the Cuban said dryly. "But that's not what I'm getting at. What lesson we need to now consider from the history of Zaire is the fact that Moise Tshombe hired European mercenaries, led by a Briton, known as Colonel 'Mad Mike' Horce. Many believe those mercenaries won most of the battles for Tshombe's forces. Mercenaries are unorthodox and by their very profession they care little about the rules of the Geneva Convention. They often succeed when ordinary soldiers would fail."

"I concur that mercenaries may fight for Kilembe," Jangwa agreed. "But so far, our comrades have only lost one small battle against Kilembe."

"We have to crush that so-called nation within four months," Perez declared. "Those are my orders. Your country is already on the verge of bankruptcy because of the fighting with the fascist South Africans, as well as the war against Savimba's forces. Angola cannot afford to conduct another long-term conflict with another enemy."

"I see." The Angolan smiled. "Yet, I suspect the four-month deadline was set by your superiors. If you fail to accomplish the goal by that time, I wonder what fate will await you. A firing squad?"

"Perhaps," Perez admitted. "But first, I'll carry out a few executions as well. If I'm going to die, I might as well make certain those who fail me pay the same price. Isn't that fair, Comrade?"

"I know better than to underestimate your ruthlessness, Colonel," Jangwa said grimly. "I just hope you plan to deal as efficiently with the enemy as you threaten to do to your allies."

"You can be sure of that," Perez stated with a grim nod.

A knock at the door drew their attention. A small, slender black man entered. He wore a jungle camouflage uniform with a spotted design, unlike the Angolan troops who generally wore green fatigues. He also wore Italian jump boots and a brown beret, items virtually never seen on Angolan troops. Perez and Jangwa would have recognized the Congolese uniform even if they hadn't already met Marcel Baridi.

"Ah! Please join us, Comrade Captain!" Perez greeted, switching to English and checking the rank patch on Baridi's shirt pocket. He thought Congolese military had to be run by idiots to adopt this odd practice. "I want to thank your government again, through you, on aiding us at this critical time against a country ideologically opposed to us both."

"Were Kilembe to go free, who knows what manner of rebellion would occur in my country?" the Congolese officer replied. "Now, to business. I've found forty-two Angolan soldiers who I believe will work well with my special operations unit, Comrade Colonel." The Congolese officer barely nodded at Jangwa, concerned only with winning the approval of the Cuban commander. "That will give us close to one hundred men in all."

"Good," Perez said. "I want them fully prepared for the mission as soon as possible. You'll supervise their training personally, Captain Baridi. I don't want any mistakes."

"No comprendo inglés," Jangwa reminded Perez.

"Dispenseme," the Cuban replied and returned to his native language of Spanish. "The captain and I were discussing the details of a plan I came up with to disrupt and divide the people of Kilembe. If it works the enemy will be fighting among themselves."

"Sounds ideal," Jangwa was forced to admit. "How do you plan to accomplish this minor miracle?"

"Miracles are only found in the mythology of religion," Perez said with a sly smile. "Our strategy is very simple. You Africans are rather divided to begin with. The Ovimbundu don't care much for the Bakongo. The Bantu are suspicious of the Beteke, and so on. We're going to use those feelings to our advantage."

"How?" the Angolan inquired.

"Captain Baridi is a Bakongo—as you mentioned earlier,'' Perez began. "Almost half the population of the People's Republic of the Congo belong to this ethnic group. But also, and more important, there are Bakongo in Kilembe, as well.''

"I wish you'd get to the point, Colonel,'' Jangwa insisted.

"Very well.'' The Cuban tapped a long ash from the tip of his cheroot. "Captain Baridi and a special unit of Congolese and Angolans are going to slip across the border into Kilembe. Some of them will dress as peasants or Bushmen. Others will wear uniforms like those worn by the Kilemban patrols. Then they will carry out acts of brutality and destruction. I'm sure they'll be very good at that. You Africans have quite a talent for that.''

"So did your Spanish ancestors,'' Jangwa sneered. "Cuban political prisons have quite a reputation, too. The Isle of Pines isn't famous for its humane treatment of inmates. But, please continue, Colonel.''

"The rest should be obvious,'' Perez said stiffly. "The Kilemban villages will believe they're being raided by Bushmen and other uncivilized savages. The backward little villages of the real Bushmen will be raided by men they will think are Kilemban troopers. Each segment of the population will rise against the other. That's the way the guerrilla raids should have been handled from the beginning. Exploit the beliefs and prejudices of the locals, and then allow them to destroy themselves.''

"What about General Zabibu and his mercenaries?'' Jangwa inquired. "Do you think they'll believe this as well?''

"What difference does that make?'' Perez chuckled. He drew deeply on the cigar and savored the smoke for a moment before he added, "The Kilembans will blame them for being unable to control the primitive elements of the republic and for allowing the local military to run amok. The citizens will probably hang Zabibu and his hired soldiers—*if* they're lucky.''

CHAPTER 12

STEVE CAINE HAD been accepted among the Bambute Pygmy tribe after the first day when he arrived with Chief Moshi. The diminutive Africans had met white men before. Many of them wore cheap plastic wristwatches, dime-store necklaces made of plastic beads, and baseball caps with most of the dye faded out. And, as Moshi had said earlier, they had a few radios through which they kept in touch a bit with the outside world.

Caine didn't know much about Pygmies, but he was aware they were nomadic people who lived by hunting and never seemed to have much interest in settling down in one place to take up farming. That was fine with Caine. The Hard Corps didn't need another group of farmers who had no idea how to defend themselves. A tribe of skilled hunters had a lot more potential.

Like most Americans, Caine had heard and read various incredible stories about Pygmies being fierce, warlike

people, and that some were cannibals. Yet, his experience
with the Katu had taught him not to believe anything about
primitive people unless it came from a first-hand source.

The tribe was only mildly surprised, in fact, when Moshi
returned with a white man. While the chief explained the
reason for Caine's visit, the Hard Corps mercenary sat by
a campfire where a number of Pgymies were eating some
sort of meat. An old man offered a strip of the meat to
Caine. Caine smiled and nodded as he accepted the charred
flesh. He chewed it and swallowed, not asking what he was
eating. He wasn't sure he wanted to know.

Caine observed the Bambute. Few of the men were over
four feet tall and most were several inches shorter. The
women were shy and stayed far from Caine, yet they made
no attempt to cover their exposed breasts.

The only dwellings were crudely constructed lean-tos
made of branches and palm leaves. Caine noticed all the
Bambute either carried weapons or had a weapon nearby.
Spears appeared to be the most popular choice. Many Pygmy
men carried spears longer than the owner was tall, but most
chose a weapon only two-and-a-half feet in length. Some
of the spears were merely sturdy poles with sharpened points
that had been hardened in fire. However, most of the weapons had metal points of brass or steel. Since Caine saw no
evidence of metal craftsmen among the Bambute, he guessed
they had probably gotten the metal spearheads through trade
with other Africans.

A few had bows made of bamboo or sapling wood with
animal gut for string. The quivers were poorly stitched animal hide with straight sticks for arrows. Caine noticed none
of the arrows had feathered ends and most appeared to have
sharpened wood points or crude arrowheads made of bone.

Several Pygmies had modern knives or machetes. The
blades were spotted with rust, but the edges appeared to be
sharp. Caine didn't see any other type of weapon. The Hard
Corps mercenary smiled as he thought of how to best impress

the Bambute without coming off as a patronizing jerk.

"My people want welcome you," Chief Moshi declared. "I have them build you a shelter."

"If possible," Caine replied, "I would rather someone showed me how to build one. Then I will show your people something useful in return."

"Okay," Moshi said, surprised by the request.

The Bambute were delighted to show Caine how to construct a lean-to. After building the shelter, Caine thanked his helpers and walked to a cluster of young bamboo reeds. He cut down a stalk with his knife and trimmed it until he had a three-foot tube of bamboo. Caine worked on it with his knife blade and ran a copper wire through the tube to make certain it was hollow.

The Pygmies watched, clearly disappointed. They had hoped the tall man with white skin and a dark beard would show them something new and useful, but it appeared he was just going to make a flute to amuse them. The Bambute had made wind instruments for centuries. Still, they figured, the white man probably meant well.

Caine completed hollowing out the bamboo tube and snapped off a four-inch section of the wire. He mentally congratulated himself for bringing the copper wire, which he hadn't intended to bring along.

The merc whittled out a small button of wood from the campfire and fitted it to one end of the small piece of wire. He made certain it would fit in the bamboo tube before he inserted the improvised dart. Caine glanced about for a target and chose the trunk of an oil palm twenty feet away. The tree wasn't close to any of the Bambute. Caine didn't want to hit one of the Pygmies and he couldn't be certain how accurate his first shot would be with an unfamiliar weapon.

Caine raised the tube to his lips, inhaled deeply, and blew into it forcibly. The dart rocketed from the wooden muzzle and struck the tree. Caine gestured at the target and invited the tribesmen to examine it. Two bold men ventured forward carefully while the others stayed back, unsure of what had happened.

"*Ona hapa!*" one of the adventurous duo cried out when he found the improvised wire-dart stuck in the tree trunk. "*Ona hapa!*"

The other men approached the tree. They stared at the dart with astonishment and talked excitedly. They smiled at Caine and nodded with approval. The mercenary nodded in reply.

"Warrior magic?" Chief Moshi inquired, looking at the bamboo tube as if it were a stone tablet with the original Ten Commandments engraved on it.

"Magic you use," Caine answered. "Very easy to make and use. You can hunt game with it. Or hunt men."

"Is better than okay," Moshi declared. "You teach us?"

"Yes," Caine replied. "I'll teach you."

Caine helped the Bambute make more blowguns and darts, some made of copper wire and some made of needle thorns and bone splinters. He instructed them in the use of the blowgun and taught them to handle the new weapons safely. By the end of his first day among the Bambute, Caine had earned not only acceptance, but respect and admiration as well.

Caine and the Pygmies continued to take turns teaching and learning from one another. Bambute hunters showed him how to safely extract poison from the root of the water hemlock found along a nearby river. The Bambute had used the poison for their arrows for centuries and now they used hemlock for the darts to their blowguns as well.

They taught Caine how to rub one's body with the leaves of an oil palm to kill the scent while tracking game. The Pygmies were extraordinary hunters. They would fearlessly stalk any quarry and even killed an occasional elephant. Armed only with spears, the diminutive hunters took advantage of their size and made full use of scant camouflage while stalking game. They had also learned to imitate the chirping of birds and insects to present the impression that all was well before they pounced on an unsuspecting zebra or gnu.

Caine showed the Bambute how to attach feathers to their arrows to improve the accuracy of the projectiles. He taught them the simple technique of attaching small branches and twigs to one's body to alter the human outline of an individual's form while creeping through bushes or hiding among tree branches. Caine instructed the Pygmies in sentry removal and taught them how to silently kill a man with garrote or knife.

With Moshi's help as translator, Caine explained fundamental strategy the Bambute would need when they confronted opponents armed with modern weapons. Caine explained this in terms the Pygmies would understand, comparing the teamwork and coordination of actions to hunting methods already used by the Bambute to deal with particularly dangerous game.

Six days after Caine joined the Bambute tribe, a group of Nilotic tribesmen approached the Pygmy camp. The Bambute recognized the visitors. They had traded with the Nilotic people in the past and the two very different cultures had discovered cooperation to be in the best interest of all involved.

The Nilotic were physically different from the Pygmies, the most obvious difference being their height. The visiting tribesmen averaged five-foot-four and taller. One Nilotic hunter stood six feet tall, his arms and shoulders well muscled above a thick chest and narrow waist.

They were not bush people in the true sense and spent less time in the tropical rain forest than the Pygmies. Perhaps this explained the rich, black, almost blue quality of the Nilotic visitors' complexion. The men of this particular tribe shaved their heads for reasons outsiders had never been able to comprehend. A number of men had also smeared their faces and chest with gray ash to form something similar to warpaint.

Two of the visitors carried rusty old bolt-action rifles, but most were armed with spears, war clubs, and machetes. The spears had brass leaf-shaped blades and the clubs were studded with metal bolts. The tall Nilotic led the group and stepped forward to address Moshi in a language with which Caine was totally unfamiliar. The Bambute chief replied in the same tongue and turned to Steve Caine.

"This man is Jiko," Moshi explained, tilting his head toward the leader of the Nilotic band. "He is a adopted son of a chief. The greatest of his tribe. Jiko's people come here from the north."

"How do I express welcome to Jiko?" Caine asked.

"No need," the Bambute chief stated. "Jiko has ask me about you. I tell him you are a friend of my people, against outsiders who want to destroy Kilembe.

"Kilembe government say it okay leave us alone," Moshi continued. "Its soldiers are supposed keep outsiders away. Let us live as we choose. That is why we help fight other soldiers."

"I understand," Caine assured him. He recalled that the Katu in Vietnam had felt much the same way when they agreed to help American servicemen against the Communists.

"Jiko says soldiers of Kilembe bad people," Moshi declared. "He says soldiers attack his village. They kill many people and took the women. Since you a Kilembe soldier, you also be bad, Steve Caine."

"Oh, shit," Caine rasped. "There's been some sort of misunderstanding, Moshi. Jiko must have mistaken terrorists for Kilemban military patrols."

"I tell him your words," the Pygmy chief replied.

Moshi translated the message to Jiko. The Nilotic warrior shouted something in an angry tone and jabbed his war lance

in the direction of Steve Caine. The Hard Corps merc didn't
think he was going to like the translation.

"Jiko says you a liar and coward," Moshi explained.
"He want you fight him with spear or club. Not with gun,
because he no know a gun. I tell him you accept."

"You did *what*?" Caine glared at the Pygmy leader.

"If you no fight, he kill you anyway," Moshi stated.
"My people no help you. This your fight, Steve Caine."

"I don't have any quarrel with this guy," the merc told
Moshi as he unbuckled his gun belt. "Jiko is mistaken about
me and he's probably wrong about the soldiers, too."

"Probably?" Moshi inquired. "You mean he be right
maybe that Kilembe soldiers attack his village?"

"Sometimes patrols take action on their own and do bad
things," Caine admitted. "No army likes to admit any of
its soldiers would do such things, but it has been known to
happen even when the army itself ordered its men to behave
otherwise."

"This be bad bad for us all." Moshi frowned. "You
want fight Jiko?"

"I don't see I have much choice," Caine replied as he
reached for a five-foot-long stave. The pole was the ideal
length to use as an improvised spear by attaching his survival
knife to the stave.

Jiko ordered his tribesmen to stay back and allow him to
deal with the white man alone. The Nilotic chanted softly
and drummed the ground with the butt-ends of spears and
rifles. Probably some sort of ritual, Caine thought. Part
cheer and part prayer for the gods to help Jiko defeat his
opponent. Caine hoped the ritual wouldn't work too well.

"You need the knife with hollow handle," Moshi reminded Caine. "You tie it to your stick end, okay?"

"No," the mercenary replied as he handed the gunbelt
and survival knife to the Pygmy chief. "I don't intend to
kill Jiko. If I can disarm him, I might get the guy to calm
down and hopefully convince the Nilotic that the Kilemban

government isn't the enemy."

"Nice," Moshi commented, shaking his head, "but stupid, too, Steve Caine, Jiko kill you. He care not if you try make him live. He still kill you."

"Thanks for the encouragement," Caine said dryly as he stepped forward.

The Bambute and Nilotic tribesmen gave the two combatants plenty of room to fight. Caine and Jiko squared off while the spectators formed a wide circle around the pair. Jiko smiled as he noticed Caine was armed only with a stave. The Nilotic warrior aimed his spear at the mercenary and slowly approached, knees bent and weight distributed on the balls of his naked feet.

Caine held the stave in both fists and waited for his opponent to launch the first attack. Jiko didn't disappoint him. The Nilotic leader faked a thrust with the spear point and quickly executed a real lunge for the mercenary's belly. Caine had not been fooled by the feint and he was ready for the attack.

The Hard Corps pro blocked the spear with the shaft of his pole. Wood cracked against wood. Jiko immediately swung a butt stroke with the other end of his spear. Caine weaved his head out of the path of the swing and jabbed an end of his stave into Jiko's chest.

The Nilotic stumbled backward from the blow. Jiko was surprised by the white stranger's skill, but he reacted well and lashed out with his spear to keep Caine at bay. He delivered an overhead slash, the sharpened edge of the brass spearhead aimed at Caine's face. The mercenary raised his stave and blocked the attack with the shaft of the pole between his fists.

Cain's boot lashed out and slammed a solid kick to his opponent's lower abdomen. Jiko groaned and doubled up from the kick. Caine quickly grabbed the shaft of the spear with one hand and chopped the stave across the Nilotic's forearms to loosen Jiko's grip on the lance. The merc yanked hard and wrenched the spear from Jiko's grasp.

He tossed the spear aside and quickly swung a low stave stroke, planning to sweep the man's legs out from under him. However, Jiko's reflexes were superb and he nimbly jumped above the whirling wood pole.

Jiko leaped forward and dived into Steve Caine. The merc lifted the stave to defend himself, but Jiko grabbed him before he could jab with the fighting stick. Strong fingers seized Caine's throat as the force of Jiko's lunge drove him backward.

Caine thrust the stave upward like a bar between his fists. The hard wood struck Jiko's wrists and broke the grip at Caine's throat. He shoved with the stave, but Jiko blocked the stroke with a shoulder and grabbed the pole to try to wrench it from Caine's hands.

Caine followed a basic principle of jujitsu. He moved with his opponent instead of trying to resist. Jiko's momentum suddenly increased and he started to lose his balance. Caine swept a boot into his ankle to complete the job. Jiko tripped and tumbled to the ground. The mercenary raised his stave overhead to simulate an attack on the fallen Nilotic's prone figure. Then he discarded the stick and stepped back from Jiko.

Surprised voices came from among the onlookers. The Nilotic tribesmen had been cheering on their champion, but now they were puzzled by Caine's actions. Although the Pygmies favored Caine, they had not voiced any encouragement for the white mercenary. Yet, all but Moshi were surprised that Caine had chosen to spare his opponent.

Jiko wasn't impressed. He scooped up a handful of dirt as he started to rise, and hurled it at Caine's face. The merc had been in too many scrapes to expect an opponent to fight by Queensberry rules. He ducked his head and shielded his eyes with a forearm to protect them from the flying dirt. Jiko charged at Caine with arms outstretched and hands aimed at the mercenary's throat.

Caine sidestepped the clumsy attack and hooked a fist into Jiko's solar plexus. The Nilotic warrior gasped as his breath heaved from his lungs. Caine smashed a heel-of-the-palm stroke to the side of his opponent's face. Jiko staggered from the blow. The Hard Corps champ grabbed the other man's right wrist and twisted hard to lock Jiko's arm.

Caine snapped a kick to Jiko's abdomen as he held the arm captive. The Nilotic's body jerked from the blow. The Hard Corps veteran nearly followed with another stroke that might kill his opponent. Jiko was clearly dazed and the poor guy was starting to vomit. Caine simply pushed him to the ground. Jiko hugged his belly and rolled onto his knees to puke helplessly into the soil.

"Chief Moshi?" Caine began, gasping for breath after the exertion and stress of the duel.

"I here," the Bambute chief assured him.

"Please tell the Nilotic tribesmen I do not wish to fight them," Caine began. "I kill my enemies without hesitation, but Jiko and his people are not enemies with me or those I work for. I would rather talk to them than shed their blood. This is a time to talk. The time to fight will come for all of us soon enough."

"I talk them, Steve Caine," Moshi replied with a grin as he began to roll himself a crude cigarette. "Now maybe they hear you."

CHAPTER 13

"SEVERAL VILLAGES AND farms claim they were attacked by Kilemban patrols," William O'Neal explained to Steve Caine after listening to the bearded merc's story. "Communications with the primitive tribes such as the Nilotics you encountered are practically nonexistent. We can only guess how many primitives have been hit by the enemy masquerading as our troops."

"Are you sure Kilemban soldiers aren't responsible?" Caine asked quietly. "The discipline and training of the military were pretty poor before we arrived. There are probably still a lot of soldiers who have a less than professional attitude about their job. They might figure pillage and rape are the fun part of war."

"I considered that possibility," O'Neal confirmed as he crossed his office to a wall map. "The reported incidents are marked on the map. None of them occurred in an area where a Kilemban patrol was on duty. Sure, a patrol might have wandered away from its proper position and attacked a village, but I don't think that happened five times in the last week.''

"Besides," Wentworth added as he poured himself a cup of tea, "I personally checked every patrol within forty miles of the first two reported incidents. Not one soldier's weapon smelled of burnt gunpowder. Not a single gun had been fired recently. They didn't do it, Steve. I doubt that the patrols were responsible for the attack on the Nilotic tribe, either.''

"Another point," O'Neal declared. "Terrorist activity by the enemy has virtually ceased. Instead, we're seeing these atrocities supposedly carried out by Kilembans against other Kilembans. The terrorists only got their ass whipped once. That wouldn't be enough to make them throw in the towel. The enemy has simply changed tactics and they're trying to get the different segments of the Kilembe Republic to fight among themselves.''

"Clever," Wentworth said, sipping the tea. "I wonder who came up with the idea? Probably a Russian or Cuban strategist in Angola.''

"It doesn't really matter who came up with the idea," Caine remarked. "It's obviously working. I managed to convince the Nilotic group led by Jiko to hold back from rallying other tribes to attack Kilemban military personnel. But there are probably other tribes and villages who are ready to start fighting back at anything in uniform. Another problem is the fact the Bambute Pygmies aren't willing to help us until this matter is resolved. After all, nobody wants to help somebody fight against an enemy if they figure they might be the target next week.''

"Do the Bambute have potential?" Wentworth inquired.

"A lot of potential," Caine confirmed. "They're accomplished hunters and experts in camouflage. They're very brave people and they'll do very well in combat. I also taught them how to use other primitive weapons such as blowguns, and I instructed them in guerrilla warfare. They learned fast. Tell ya something else, sir. We *don't* want them for enemies.''

"I don't know if it'll do any good to tell the Bambute or the Nilotic what we've found out about the attacks on the villages and farms," O'Neal said, taking a pack of cigarettes from his pocket. "They've got no reason to believe us. Do you think you can keep a lid on them for a while, Steve?''

"For a while," Caine answered. "But I don't know how long they'll wait before they either decide to haul ass or turn against us."

"Are you sure you'll be safe with them?" Wentworth asked.

"Is anybody safe, Lieutenant?" Caine replied. "I don't think I'll be in any greater danger from the Bambute or the Nilotic than any of us are from the enemy or from an uprising by pissed-off farmers.''

"I see," Wentworth said stiffly. "Well, I'm sure you'll be careful. However, I suggest you remember that you are a major now. You've been promoted to a field-grade position of authority and you're expected to conduct yourself with a bit more detachment from the troops. By the way, you might also remember I'm a lieutenant colonel now."

"Whatever you say, Lieutenant," Caine said with a wry grin. "If you two don't need me for anything, I'd better be going.''

"Just one minute—" Wentworth began.

"Hell, Jim," O'Neal said, trying not to smile. "Let the man get back to his job.''

Caine left the office. Wentworth stared at the door and shook his head with dismay. O'Neal blew a smoke ring toward the ceiling and watched it dissolve as the current of the electric fan caught it in mid-flight.

"Hey, Jim," the Hard Corps commander began. "Don't forget why Zabibu gave us these promotions. Our present ranks are just honorary and we're not really colonels and majors.''

"Do you know how long I've been a first lieutenant?''

Wentworth asked, a trace of disappointment in his voice. "I never thought I'd spend the rest of my life with that rank after I'd graduated West Point with honors."

"Hell, we're mercenaries, Jim," O'Neal told him. "It doesn't matter if we call ourselves lieutenants, captains, colonels, or field marshals. Come on, Jim. We don't really hold any rank in any regular military anymore. Up until Zabibu pinned birdies and oak leaves on our collars, none of the Hard Corps had worn any sort of rank insignia since 'Nam."

"I know," Wentworth nodded wearily. "I know it's silly, but I . . . well, I rather like the idea of being a colonel."

"You are a colonel right now," O'Neal assured him. "But don't try to be something you aren't. Especially, don't try to change Caine and Fanelli. They know how to do their jobs. Their style is different from yours, but they're still good men and they've never let us down. The Hard Corps ain't broke, so don't try to fix it. Okay?"

"Okay," Wentworth agreed, managing a weak smile. "By the way, I haven't seen Fanelli today. Is he still trying to whip up homemade explosives in that little mad-scientist lab?"

"He and the chemists already finished making a bunch of a gelatin explosive," O'Neal explained. "I don't quite understand what it is, but Joe said it's sort of like tetryl with a stabilizing agent. Supposedly, it'll work well in grenades and shaped charges."

"When it comes to demolitions, Joe knows what he's talking about," Wentworth had to admit. "After all, he made land mines out of bat dung in Bolivia. I don't know anyone else who can make that claim—not that I know anyone who'd want to."

"Well, I sent Joe out with a patrol to the northwest portion of Kilembe," O'Neal continued. "That's where the last villages and farms reported being attacked by the phony patrols. Maybe Joe can find some evidence to prove our people didn't do it."

"Caine is better at reading sign and tracking," Wentworth commented. "He would have been a better choice to send for that sort of mission than Fanelli."

"I know," O'Neal admitted. "But we need Caine to work with the Pygmies. None of the rest of us could begin to form the kind of rapport with primitive people that Caine can establish with them. Of course, Fanelli has some good trackers with his group. They should be able to compensate for any skills Joe lacks."

"I hope that means someone in his group has a little common sense," Wentworth said with gruffness, trying to conceal the genuine concern he felt for Fanelli.

Joe Fanelli was pissed off. A map of the area claimed there was a road extending across the northwest portion of the country. *Some road*, Fanelli thought sourly. It was a goddamn dirt path, which had been neglected for God knows how long. The region was located in a tropical rain forest in some godforsaken former part of Zaire.

Grass, ferns, and weeds had grown up through the soil of the road. Tangles of vines and brush formed solid barriers in the path of the three surplus U.S. Army jeeps. Several men walked ahead of the vehicles. Three men were familiar with the area and remained well ahead of the others, scouting for signs of trouble. The rest concentrated on clearing the brush in the road to cut a path for the vehicles. They hacked away at the vegetation with machetes and pushed foliage out of the way. It was hard work and soldiers took turns with the unpleasant chore to avoid completely exhausting the men involved with the task.

Fanelli crushed a mosquito against his neck and cursed under his breath. He hoped the guys up ahead knew what they were doing. Between the jeeps and the dudes thrashing about in the brush, the enemy could hear them coming half a mile away. A couple of other men brought up the rear of the convoy in case enemy forces tried to ambush them from behind.

"You sure they got towns around here, Lieutenant?" Fanelli asked Lieutenant Mgawa, his primary translator.

"Oh, yes," Mgawa confirmed with an energetic nod. He was a young intellectual, more accustomed to libraries than jungles. "There are hills to the north. Coffee is grown there and cotton is harvested in the plains below them."

"I'll take your word for it," Fanelli told him, unable to see why anyone would try to grow anything in a dense mass of overgrown crabgrass.

"We will soon reach a village only a few kilometers away, Major," Mgawa assured him. "Please be patient."

"Okay," Fanelli replied, lighting a cigarette. "Thanks, Lieutenant."

"Maybe we come across some of those bandits," the young officer remarked. "That would be very bad for them. Yes, Major?"

"Might not be so good for us either," Fanelli stated. He had met eager young guys like this in 'Nam. They were real good at getting themselves killed.

Fanelli smiled at a private joke as he recalled that he had once been one of those eager young guys who could hardly wait to get into the bush and get his first taste of combat. He'd gone off to war to show everybody back in Jersey that Joe Fanelli was a tough little fucker who won himself some medals in combat.

He figured he'd come back from the war as a hero. Instead, he almost got killed and wound up with a medical discharge under honorable conditions. Sure he got some medals in the process, but there were no parades waiting for him when he got home. Of course, there wouldn't be any parades this time either. Mercenaries don't get parades. They fight in dirty little wars that regular governments don't want to get involved in. They take on nasty missions with a high risk factor that nobody else wants to stick their necks out for. Still, it was what he'd chosen for a living and he really couldn't think of anything he'd rather be doing.

Suddenly, Lieutenant Mgawa screamed and staggered away from Fanelli. The shaft of an arrow trembled as it protruded from Mgawa's left forearm. The crimson-drenched arrowhead jutted from the opposite side of his arm. The lieutenant tumbled into the back of a jeep and slumped to his knees, clutching the wounded limb.

"Shit!" Fanelli exclaimed as he yanked an M-16 assault rifle from his shoulder and ducked behind the vehicle. "Everybody down!"

The mercenary's warning was too late for a Kilemban soldier who received an arrow in the center of his chest. The man uttered a long ugly groan and fell to the ground as other troops dived for cover behind vehicles or in the thick foliage surrounding the road. Another soldier screamed and tumbled into the open, the shaft of a spear quivering between his shoulder blades.

A naked figure stirred among the elephant grass behind the man who'd been speared in the back. Fanelli swung his M-16 at the shape, flicked the selector switch to full auto, and opened fire. The ambusher cried out as three 5.56-mm rounds ripped into his flesh. The attacker fell from view as an arrow shrieked past Fanelli's left ear. It struck the frame of the jeep, the arrowhead buried under the metal skin.

Fanelli's guts twisted with stark terror, but his reflexes took control. He whirled and scanned the trees and foliage for sign of his attacker. Another man lurked among the limbs of an okoume mahogany tree. He was clad only in something that looked like a jockstrap made of antelope skin. The figure fumbled with a bow, trying to draw and fire an arrow.

The Hard Corps pro's movements were swift and accurate. Fanelli raised his rifle and triggered a three-round blast into the tree limbs. The archer howled with pain as a bullet tore into his shoulder. Another bullet splintered his bow and singed his rib cage, and the third slug burrowed into the tree trunk next to the guy's elbow. The impact of the high-velocity projectile in his deltoid still did the job. The ambusher was tugged off-balance by the force and slipped from the branches.

The enemy bowman plunged from the tree and crashed to earth fifteen feet below. Fanelli figured the guy had probably survived, but he wouldn't present any immediate threat. The merc searched the jungle for more opponents, peering through the sights of his assault rifle.

Suddenly attackers appeared from all directions. Dark figures rose from the bushes and elephant grass. Most launched arrows at the patrol. A few hurled spears while others banged the shafts of lances or war clubs against the hard surface of wooden shields. The latter effort was only intended to distract the soldiers while the others propelled crude projectiles at the group.

Several of Fanelli's men cried out in pain as arrows pierced flesh. One soldier collapsed with a spear hanging from his belly, the brass tip buried in his intestines. He fell forward and landed on the end of the shaft. This drove the spear deeper. The man shrieked once and mercifully fainted.

However, Fanelli's men fought back. Rifles chattered out sprays of full-auto fire. Enemy bowmen dropped their weapons and fell, bare flesh torn and bloodied by multiple bullet holes. Some of the henchmen who'd only beaten their shields to distract the troops were also targets of the desperate rifle fire. The brush rustled and quivered as wounded and dying figures fell to the green floor of the jungle.

An arrow passed over Fanelli's bowed head, tugging the boonie-hat from his skull. His spine quaked with icy fear as he shifted the rifle to aim in the general direction that the arrow had come from. He couldn't see the enemy among the dense elephant grass and clusters of yard-high ferns.

God, it was like 'Nam! Invisible opponents hidden in the bush. Fanelli sprayed the rounds from his weapon, blasting bullets into the foliage without truly aiming. There was no definite target to aim at. Goddamn M-16 wasn't the greatest choice for shooting into a fucking jungle either. The 5.56-

mm slug was too small, too apt to tumble instead of penetrate when it hit a clump of dense vegetation.

Fanelli wished he had a .45-caliber Thompson sub-machine gun. No, he thought, his mind working as fast as the full-auto bullets spitting from the rifle; he needed a goddamn *M-60* machine gun. Big, bad mother with a bipod mount and a couple of thousand rounds of 7.62-mm cartridges belt-fed into the monster chopper. *Yeah, man*. That sucker would blow the shit outa every friggin' Charlie Cong in the bush.

''Fuckin'-A!'' Fanelli shouted as if bellowing a battle cry; he emptied the M-16 magazine, firing the last rounds into the enemies' hiding place.

Two figures bobbed into view. One man was naked from the waist up and held a small bamboo bow in his fist. The other was dressed as a Kilemban soldier, both hands clamped over his bullet-shattered face. The pair appeared for less than a heartbeat, both splattered with blood and clearly dying. Then they toppled behind the screen of tall grass and taunting plant-life.

''Oh, Christ!'' Fanelli exclaimed, eyes wide with horror. The crimson-stained uniform of one of the targets burned a nightmare image into his brain.

I shot one of my own men, Fanelli thought, stunned by the terrible, gut-churning sight. *How the hell did he get over there with the enemy? What the fuck difference does that make? I killed him . . .*

A large figure charged from the brush. The muscular shape wore only a tanned loincloth, a necklace of crocodile teeth, and an ebony birthday suit. He wielded a wooden shield in one fist and a war club in the other. The latter was roughly two feet long with a thick knotted end: an African shillelagh in the hands of a homicidal madman.

Fanelli raised his empty M-16 as the attacker swung his club. Wood struck metal and the rifle popped free of Fanelli's grasp. The tough merc jumped to his feet and dodged a vicious backhand sweep. The cudgel barely missed the end of his nose. The attacker hissed like a snake through the clenched white teeth that bisected his wide dark features.

Gunshots and screams assaulted Fanelli's ears, but he barely noticed. At that moment the rest of the world was an illusion. All that existed was Joe Fanelli and the big bad dude who intended to bash his brains in. The only reality was survival.

Fanelli considered reaching for his .45 Colt, but he realized the other guy could take his head off before he could get the pistol past leather. The African smiled, confident of victory as he raised his club for another swing.

Joe Fanelli kicked him hard right in the center of his antelope briefs.

The African gasped and doubled up from the pain in his ruptured manhood. Fanelli grabbed the guy's wrist and twisted hard. The war club fell from the man's fingers, but he quickly lashed out with his shield. The wood plank struck Fanelli on a shoulder and drove him back into the rear of the jeep. The African assailant bent over to reach for his fallen club.

Fanelli swung a boot to the guy's face. The kick straightened the attacker's back and sent his head bobbing as if trying to place the back of his skull between his own shoulder blades. This motherfucker was *tough*, Fanelli concluded.

The Hard Corps merc rammed a right hook to the African's solar plexus and tagged him on the side of the jaw with a left. The man staggered slightly and swung his shield at Fanelli. The American dodged the attack and hammered his left fist across his opponent's elbow joint. The blow to the ulna nerve jarred loose the shield from the other man's grasp.

Fanelli had him now. He jabbed a left to the guy's jaw and watched the African's features dance from the impact of his knuckles. Blood leaked from the aggressor's nose and mouth, yet he was still on his feet. Fanelli hit him with another left jab and followed with a hard right cross. The man's knees buckled and he crashed unconscious to the ground.

A uniformed figure stepped from the jungle. Fanelli reached for his pistol, but held his hand frozen on the holster when he recognized the uniform and insignia of a Kilemban sergeant. The sergeant smiled and raised a Soviet PPS submachine gun and pointed it at Fanelli.

Three shots roared, the sound tumbling together as the reports erupted rapidly. The sergeant convulsed from the impact of two bullets in the chest and one in the center of his grinning mouth. The PPS clattered to the ground and its owner fell lifeless beside it.

Fanelli turned to see Lieutenant Mgawa leaning against the frame of the jeep. The arrow was still lodged in the young officer's left forearm, but he held a Smith & Wesson .38 Special in his right fist. Mgawa lowered his revolver and wearily returned it to the holster on his hip. Fanelli realized the fighting had ceased.

"Thanks, Lieutenant," the merc declared as he helped Mgawa climb into the jeep. "I owe you one."

"It was nothing, sir," Mgawa said, his face coated with a layer of sweat. "That man was not one of ours . . ."

"I figured that," Fanelli agreed. "None of our guys were packin' Russian hardware."

"Major?" a Kilemban sergeant—a real one this time—approached Fanelli. "Sir, we have taken four of the savages prisoner. Do we take them back, or kill them right here and now?"

"You ain't gonna murder nobody while I'm in charge," Fanelli said sharply. "And get a medic over here for Lieutenant Mgawa. How many others are hurt?"

"Several," the sergeant replied. "We lost six men and a couple of others don't look like they'll survive, sir. Do we turn back?"

"Yeah," Fanelli confirmed. "I think the others will wanna know about this."

CHAPTER 14

GENERAL ZABIBU STARED at the column of corpses placed on the parade field. Some were soldiers killed on patrol. Most were slain enemies. The majority were clad only in loincloths and jewelry. A few were dressed in Kilemban uniforms.

"Are you *certain* these were terrorists?" Zabibu asked, gesturing at the bodies of the bogus soldiers.

"Hey, the fuckers tried to kill us, General," Fanelli replied, clearly annoyed. "Ain't that good enough evidence?"

"None of these men had dogtags, Jacob," James Wentworth told Zabibu. "In fact, they didn't carry any sort of identification. They carried nothing but weapons, ammo, and some supplies. None of the other men in your military recognize these guys. Now, I don't know if one would technically call these fellows terrorists, but they sure as hell weren't our people."

"Thank God," Fanelli commented, recalling how he'd felt when he'd thought he'd killed one of his own men.

"What about these other bodies?" Zabibu asked, referring to the dead men in traditional dress.

"They're phonies, too," Wentworth assured him as he knelt by one of the dead men and grabbed an ankle. "Look at this, Jacob."

He raised the dead man's foot. Zabibu examined it. The sole was barely calloused and the toenails had been recently clipped. The general had known enough tribesmen to realize the feet belonged to a man who had generally worn shoes or boots.

"I see what you mean." Zabibu nodded.

"If that's not good enough," Wentworth continued as he pointed at another dead man, "that one is still wearing a wristwatch. A Czech wristwatch, to be exact. A few others over here are also wearing items made in Iron Curtain countries. A couple even have Cuban army boots."

"There is little doubt these men were invaders from Angola," Zabibu said. "They disguised themselves as Nilotic tribesmen or whatever to try to convince us the patrol was attacked by hostile tribes within our republic. But carrying out a full attack on the patrol was very careless. They should know that close inspection of their garments—"

"I imagine they originally planned to just hit and run," Wentworth interrupted, fondling the hilt of the WWII samurai sword thrust in his gun belt. "The fellows dressed as our troops were probably along to help bail them out in case the situation required more firepower than bows and arrows could provide. However, I believe their plans changed when they discovered Fanelli among the patrol."

"*Major* Fanelli," the merc from Jersey commented. Fanelli didn't really care much about his honorary rank, but he knew it aggravated Wentworth.

"When they saw a white man in the group," Wentworth continued, deciding to ignore Fanelli's remark, "they probably suspected he was a mercenary or CIA or whatever they think we might be. But obviously, they had no idea what Fanelli is *really* like."

"That's cute, Colonel," Fanelli snickered. "Fact is, we dished out more than the bastards were ready to handle. Considering how little time we've had to work with the Kilembans, they handled themselves damn good in a fire-fight too."

"You men have worked miracles upon our army," Zabibu said gratefully as he watched a company of soldiers rigidly marching in step to the cadence call of a senior sergeant. "Last month this group looked more like a collection of derelicts. You know, we'd lost every encounter with the enemy until you arrived."

"We couldn't have accomplished anything without the spirit and cooperation of your people, Jacob," Wentworth told him. "They deserve a lot of credit, too."

"But we deserve more money," Fanelli muttered in a voice too low for Zabibu to detect.

Wentworth glared at Fanelli. But Zabibu was still watching the soldiers march along the parade field. He was thinking about the future of his country, a future which remained grim. The Republic of Kilembe was as surrounded by hostile forces as ever.

"Hello, General," William O'Neal greeted as he crossed the parade field to join the others. "Jim fill you in on everything we've learned about the masquerade the other side has been playing?"

"People have been killed, Colonel O'Neal," Zabibu replied with a trace of disapproval in his tone.

"It's all a game." O'Neal shrugged. "Half of all marriages are a failure, but people still go out and tie the knot. Insurance companies bet that you'll live long enough to pay enough installments so they'll make a profit. Banks, governments, everybody gambles with people's lives at one time or other. When you think about it, war may be the only honest game in town."

"I suppose everyone needs a philosophy," Zabibu said tersely. "I find yours a bit cynical, Colonel. I suppose that's part of being a professional mercenary."

"Mercenaries don't start wars," O'Neal replied. "We just fight 'em after guys who run governments—guys like you—get 'em started. That's okay with me. That's my job and as long as I figure I'm fighting for the right side, I don't worry about it."

"Even if it's not the winning side?" Zabibu asked.

"You haven't lost yet, General," O'Neal replied. "Luckily, the other side fucked up when they jumped Fanelli's patrol. I've been on the radio talkin' to some troops in the field. We're going to encourage every village, farm, or tribe with more than two huts to send somebody down here to see these bodies for themselves. I want them all to know what kind of shit the other side has pulled."

"How will that prevent this from happening in the future?" Zabibu asked.

"We'll set up passwords with civilian communities," O'Neal answered. "Change them from time to time and make sure all military personnel know the right phrase before they head toward a town. More and more civilians will be taking fundamental combat-training courses from military personnel. They'll get to know the guys, like neighborhoods used to know the cops walkin' the beat on their block. They'll learn to recognize real soldiers from the phonies and learn to trust 'em in the process."

"Not to mention the fact they'll also be able to help fight the invaders in the future," Wentworth added.

"But there still aren't enough weapons or ammunition to arm all the soldiers, let alone the civilians," Zabibu reminded the mercs.

"We're going to see about changing that situation," O'Neal answered. "So far we've been on the defensive. It's about time we took the offensive."

"Offensive?" Zabibu frowned. "I trust you realize that officially Kilembe isn't technically at war with anyone. However, if you launch a military offensive against our neighboring countries, you will undoubtedly give them the justification to invade us. There's no way we could survive an all-out assault.''

"Don't worry," O'Neal assured him. "We don't plan to start a full-scale war. What we have in mind is just giving the other side a taste of their own tactics. After all, they've been able to get away with terrorist raids because your government hasn't been able to prove they're responsible. Up till now, that is. You've noticed the enemy corpses have a lot of goodies from Communist countries? Everything from Soviet-made firearms to compasses imported from East Germany.''

"I've noticed," Zabibu confirmed. "I suppose that is proof that the Angolans are involved.''

"Are any Western reporters in Kilembe?" Wentworth asked.

"Quite a few," Zabibu answered. "Most are staying at the Hotel Cosmopolite. It is the only decent hotel in our country. I believe a few are Americans, though most are from Europe.''

"Ordinarily we try to avoid those folks, but let's take advantage of them now," O'Neal declared. "Get 'em down here and let them take photographs of these bodies. Just tell 'em the truth, but don't mention us. You won't get more favorable media coverage if they know you hired a team of professional mercenaries, and we sure as hell don't need the publicity either.''

"Do you think this will do any good?" Zabibu asked.

"Every country is sensitive to media exposure," Wentworth told him. "After all, look at Zaire. You say it won't attack you because it's afraid of bad press. While I don't fully buy that, I must admit that it's been true up to now.''

"Angola won't run for cover," O'Neal said, "but they'll be reluctant to launch more terrorist attacks until they can figure out how to avoid getting burned if their plans don't work out. Won't win the war, but it'll buy us some time.''

"Time is something we can use," Zabibu said with a smile. "The United Nations autumn session convenes two months from now. The General Assembly is to take up several matters, including the possiblity of recognition of the Republic of Kilembe as an independent nation and its subsequent admission to the world body."

"That could help," O'Neal stated. "When's your national election supposed to take place?"

"Next month," Zabibu replied. "I'm trying to get United Nations observers here to witness the fair elections of candidates who are running for office in Kilembe—including the president. Democracy, my friends. For the first time, the people in this land will be able to vote in a multiparty election and have a voice in their own government."

"That could mean the United Nations will also send some peacekeeping troops and station them along the borders, if we can convince the world that Angola's been responsible for terrorist activity here," Wentworth commented.

"Be that as it may," O'Neal said. "I say we should concentrate on press coverage of the terrorists' origins and try to get the UN to send observers to oversee the election. None of the enemies—including the Russians and the Cubans—will want to try anything while Kilembe is crawling with UN observers. About all we can do in the meantime is try to beef up our troops, continue training, and try to handle whatever the other side throws at us."

"And take a little shopping trip into their territory," Fanelli added with a grin.

"I still have some serious reservations about you gentlemen carrying out some sort of raid in Angola," Zabibu insisted. "And, of course, Zaire is totally off-limits. But even if it were safe to do so, we haven't enough intelligence information about Angola."

"We've got a number of prisoners to question," O'Neal explained. "I've made sure we've got competent people guarding them. The men in charge have orders not only to keep the prisoners from trying to escape, but also watch for any sign that a prisoner might be trying to communicate with a guy in another cell or attempt to commit suicide.''

"I hope you made sure none of 'em plan to torture information outa the prisoners," Fanelli remarked. "A couple of guys in my patrol wanted to carve up our captives five minutes after we got 'em. Lieutenant Mgawa helped me get them under control before they could start whittlin' away on those dudes. Mgawa tells me they just wanted to get a little revenge."

"Mgawa sounds like a good man," O'Neal remarked.

"He is," Fanelli confirmed. "He also speaks at least four languages and he held up well enough under stress to handle a gun after he got wounded. You'll find him in the clinic with his arm bandaged up. I think he oughta be promoted to captain. Fuckin' guy saved my life."

"We'll promote him anyway," Wentworth observed.

"Caine ought to be back any minute now," O'Neal commented, checking his wristwatch. "When he returns, we'll start questioning the prisoners."

"Is Major Caine an expert in such interrogations?" Zabibu inquired.

"Let's just say he has a way with people," the Hard Corps commander replied.

CHAPTER 15

STEVE CAINE DIDN'T have to say a word. He entered a drab stone cell without windows, a cot, or commode. James Wentworth III and a lone prisoner were already inside the cell. The prisoner was naked and chained hand and foot. Caine sat cross-legged on the floor and unrolled an oil-skin cloth which contained a small brass dish with charcoal, a pair of pliers, and his survival knife.

"He tells me he's from the Congo," Wentworth said. "He speaks French—not Portuguese. Do you realize what this means?"

Caine looked at Wentworth thoughtfully for a moment before replying. "The People's Republic of the Congo? Are they involved?"

"Apparently so," Wentworth said. "They feel ideologically committed to helping Angola, according to this prisoner. I also suspect that they're worried their own Bakongo population will be attracted to Kilembe by the Bakongo population here."

"That adds a whole new dimension," Caine said, returning to the dish with charcoal.

"*Qu'est-ce que ça veut dire?*" the prisoner asked nervously.

"*Comment?*" Wentworth replied, addressing the Congolese captive. "You want to know what my friend has? You'll find out soon enough. It's sort of a living nightmare."

"*Je ne comprends pas,*" the prisoner said, fearfully watching Caine set fire to the charcoal in the dish.

"Oh, you'll understand everything when my friend starts working on you," Wentworth assured him. "You see, he learned all about torture while in the Orient. Pressure points, nerve centers, all that sort of thing. A kind of vicious form of acupuncture. They've really made quite a science of inflicting pain."

"*Cochons!*" the prisoner hissed, and spat at Wentworth. "I will tell you nothing!"

"How very brave you are," Wentworth remarked, glancing down at the saliva on his uniform trousers. "But you will talk. My friend specializes in this sort of thing. Remarkable what he can do with such simple tools. He generally likes to start with the feet. Thousands of nerve endings in the feet. Sometimes he uses the pliers to crush the joints in the toes and then inserts a knife blade or needle after it's been heated. Digs it into the marrow of the broken bone."

The prisoner shivered and he looked away from Wentworth. The mercenary XO realized the guy was thinking about the threat of torture. That was the idea. They wanted to break him down without having to touch him.

"This is the ideal torture," Wentworth continued. "It can go on for hours without any risk of killing the subject. Even days. But we don't have that much time. If you don't talk after about three hours or so of toe-torture, my friend will move on to other things. He might decide to start pulling out your teeth with the pliers. Or maybe yank out your fingernails—one by one. He might get the blade of his knife white hot and jam it into your armpits. Or into your rectum."

Screams of agony erupted from the corridor outside the cell. The prisoner sat up, his eyes wide and his lips quivering with terror.

"Sounds like some of my other friends are working on your comrades," Wentworth said. "They'll all talk eventually. I'm sure you know them better than I do. Who do you think will last the longest? Who will crack first?"

"You go to hell," the prisoner said through chattering teeth.

"You'll go there first, but only after you've experienced our exquisite torments," Wentworth told him. "You'll *wish* you were dead. You may try to kill yourself, but we'll stop you. If the torture continues tomorrow then my friend will have to use techniques that might be too much for your heart. One of his subjects in South America went into massive shock after he crushed the fellow's testicles with his pliers. Ripped one of them out and had to sew the skin to keep the man from bleeding to death. Anyway, poor bastard went into shock and never regained consciousness really. He moaned and slobbered like a wounded beast for five days before he died. Not quite sure what he died of. Probably an infection that got out of control."

"Shut up," the prisoner urged, his voice as soft as a prayer.

"The real pity is no one will know about your ordeal," Wentworth said with a sigh. "We won't put you in a cell with your comrades. In fact we'll probably take you back across Zaire to the Congo if you're still alive. If you're crippled, blind, and castrated you'll just have to hope one of your border patrol officers takes pity on you and puts a bullet in your head when he finds you dragging your body across the jungle floor. Maybe the hyenas will get you first. Of course, if you're still in one piece you can go back and tell them whatever story you want."

"How do I know you won't just kill me if I talk?" the prisoner demanded.

"We don't have anything against you personally,"

Wentworth said. It was one of the few truthful statements he'd made since he'd entered the cell. "We don't want to kill you. Taking you to the border won't be any trouble."

"What about my comrades?" the guy asked.

"A couple of them have already told us information about the location of an Angolan military base with a large armory and motor pool," Wentworth said. "My friend used some fundamental bone-scraping to break them down. All we want from you is similar information so we can cross-check it to see if anyone is lying to us. After that, all of your comrades will be released—either at the Zaire border or in Angola. So far, none of your friends have been seriously harmed, although one or two may have to use crutches to get across the border."

"I don't know if I can trust you," the prisoner said, confused and more frightened of Caine's silence than he was of Wentworth's threats.

Steve Caine turned his head to gaze at the prisoner. His dark eyes revealed no emotion. His expression was blank, indifferent to the plight of the prisoner. The Congolese captive was sick with fear as he stared into Caine's cold fish-eye gaze. He didn't want this man to touch him. He didn't want this creature with the eyes of a corpse in the same room with him.

"I'll talk to you, Colonel," the prisoner announced in an unsteady voice, "but get that one out of here."

"*Un instant, s'il vous plaît,*" Wentworth replied. He turned to Steve Caine and addressed him in English. "Our friend would like to speak with me privately."

Caine simply nodded and gathered up his instruments. He stepped from the cell and closed the door. Caine heard the prisoner's voice rattling out a string of sentences in French. He smiled slightly and walked down the corridor to an open doorway. Loud moans and occasional shrieks of pain still issued from the room within.

"None of you guys have a chance of a career as an opera singer," Caine announced as he appeared in the doorway.

Joe Fanelli and two Kilemban men who'd volunteered to "bellow and groan as if suffering the torments of the damned" sat in comfortable armchairs with a card table loaded with beer and ashtrays. Fanelli glanced up at Caine and turned to the two "moaners." He stroked a finger across his throat to signal for them to stop.

"Did he buy it?" Fanelli inquired.

"Lock, stock, and bullshit," Caine replied with a nod. "He's in there babbling about something or other. Wentworth has a small tape recorder hidden inside his jacket, so we should have a pretty clear record of all the details. I just hope he tells us something useful."

"Was he scared?" one of the Kilembans asked with an unpleasant smile on his face.

"Of course he was scared," Caine replied, fixing his special lifeless stare on the man's face. "I figure he had a right to be scared. I don't really find that to be funny. The man believed he might be tortured or killed. He believed his friends were being tortured in other cells. Is that funny?"

"No, Major," the man answered, suddenly understanding and going quiet. "I don't think it's funny at all."

"You didn't have to hurt the guy, did you, Steve?" Fanelli inquired, raising a beer bottle to his lips.

"No," Caine declared as he grabbed Joe's wrist before Fanelli could drink from the bottle. "Mind if I take this?"

"Yeah," Fanelli said tensely, glaring up at Caine. "I mind. But take it anyway."

"Could you guys go outside for a while?" Caine asked the two Kilembans. "Major Fanelli and I gotta talk about something private."

The two men didn't need to be told twice. They left the room and headed for the stairs. Caine closed the door and placed the beer bottle back on the table.

"I'm not gonna lecture you, Joe," he stated in a stern, even voice. "You know you're an alcoholic and you know what happens when you start drinking again."

"Guess you guys won't ever let me live down that slip-up

I made in Bolivia,'' Fanelli said with a frown.

"We need you sober, buddy,'' Caine told him. "You wanna fall off the wagon, you do it when we get back to the States.''

"Fuckin-A,'' Fanelli agreed. "Well, you gonna tell the old man about the beer?''

"What kind of NCO you think I am?'' Caine asked. "Think I'd rat on a fellow sergeant? To an officer, no less?''

"I think you'd tell O'Neal if you figured I was a danger to the mission,'' Fanelli said. "And I wouldn't blame you, Steve.''

"You gonna leave the fire water alone?'' Caine asked.

Fanelli shoved a boot into the card table and kicked it over. Bottles shattered and beer spilled across the floor. Fanelli looked down at the mess with satisfaction.

"That felt good,'' he declared.

"You really are a crazy bastard,'' Caine said, shaking his head. "Go get a cup of coffee or something. I'll hang around here in case Wentworth needs any help.''

"I'd better make sure my moaners don't wander off,'' Fanelli commented. "We'll need 'em when we gotta repeat our little performance.''

Wentworth emerged from the cell at the end of the corridor. Fanelli and Caine heard the heavy metal door close. They stepped into the hall as the Hard Corps officer approached.

"Learn anything interesting, Lieutenant?' Fanelli asked. "Oops, sorry. I mean, Colonel.''

"Oh, that's all right,'' Wentworth replied wearily. "Like Bill said, these ranks are just make-believe anyway. The prisoner told me about a military base about five kilometers southeast of the Angola border. Sounds like it's just what we—''

Wentworth stared into the room. He raised his eyebrows when he saw the table lying on its side surrounded by broken glass and spilled beer.

"What happened here?'' Wentworth asked.

"Oh, I just thought I'd make the room look more like an NCO club," Fanelli explained with a chuckle.

"I don't think I'll even bother to ask why you did this," Wentworth stated, shaking his head slowly.

"Just as well," Fanelli replied cheerfully. "I don't think you'd understand it anyhow."

CHAPTER 16

THE HARD CORPS trekked slowly through the tropical rain forest in the dark of night. Along with them were five Kilemban troops and three Bambute Pygmies. The Kilembans had been chosen for this mission because they knew the area.

Steve Caine seemed quite at home with the jungle. He carried a bamboo bow with a quiver of arrows slung over his shoulder. Caine was also armed with a blowgun, .45 Colt pistol, and his ever-present survival knife. He did not carry a rifle or grenades.

However, William O'Neal and Joe Fanelli had more faith in their M-16s than Caine's primitive weapons. Fanelli also carried some makeshift explosives in a backpack. He seemed perfectly calm about carrying enough blasting power to blow away half a city block, but none of the others shared his faith in the stability of the improvised demolitions. Everybody hoped Fanelli's backpack didn't stop a bullet—and, if it did, they hoped they wouldn't be near him when it happened.

James Wentworth III was armed with an FAL 7.62-mm rifle with a Bushnell scope and a crude silencer made of a foot-long section of pipe and steel wool. He also carried the samurai sword. Some of the others, including O'Neal, had machetes, but they used the jungle knives sparingly because they had now crossed the Angolan border and entered hostile territory. Any telltale sounds could betray their presence to the enemy.

The Kilembans were armed with M-16 assault rifles, handguns, and a few Soviet-made F-1 hand grenades confiscated from slain terrorists. The Bambute tribesmen carried bows, arrows, blowguns, and spears. The diminutive warriors never seemed to stop grinning. They behaved as if they were going to a picnic instead of launching a raid on an enemy base. O'Neal wondered if bringing the Pygmies along might prove to be a big mistake.

Maybe a fatal one.

O'Neal had other concerns about the mission. Thanks to the interrogation techniques of Wentworth and Caine, they had learned the location of the Angolan military base. Three prisoners had given them information about the base, but they differed on statements about details such as estimated troop strength, security of the installation, and storage of weapons and ammo. This wasn't uncommon because individuals remember "facts" differently and often get details confused under stress. One or more of them may have also lied about details in the hope of fouling up the Hard Corps' plan to hit the place.

Wentworth and Caine had interrogated the other prisoners, but two of them had been ordered into the field right out of a base in the Congo and knew absolutely nothing about Angola. Two other prisoners had guessed what the Hard Corps was up to and refused to say anything.

O'Neal wasn't worried about being unable to find the base, but he wished he could be sure about what the hell they would be facing when they got there. He tried to push such notions from his mind as they crept through the jungle. Soon they'd find out for themselves—the hard way.

The Hard Corps wished they had some night-vision equipment. Starlite viewers or infrared scopes for rifles, something to assist the naked eye in the near-total darkness. Caine didn't seem to mind, but he was used to creeping around in the night like a fox hunting for sleeping quail. The other three mercenaries didn't care much for the fact that they couldn't see more than vague shapes in the darkness. They wished they could see if there was a black mamba coiled on the ground near their feet or if the ferns in front of them were crawling with scorpions.

The Hard Corps' search finally paid off. Beyond the jungle, in a savannah of tall grass, short bushes, and an occasional tree, they found the Angolan military base.

It was roughly a mile in diameter. O'Neal strained his eyes as he peered through a pair of Zeiss binoculars, once again wishing he had a Starlite viewer to penetrate the darkness. Several buildings stood on the enemy compound. Most were large wooden structures, probably billets for troops. O'Neal stifled a curse. *There could be more than four hundred troops housed in those buildings!*

The motor pool contained at least ten trucks and six Land Rovers. O'Neal recognized the trucks as Soviet-made ZIL-151 four-ton vehicles, similar to the army trucks favored by the NVA back in Vietnam. A huge tanker truck was also parked in the motor pool, no doubt filled with hundreds of gallons of gasoline.

The fuel was also used to power the electrical generators on the base. Floodlights hung from trees and O'Neal noticed lights in the windows of several buildings. The Angolans were clearly building a permanent base in the area. They might even have plans of constructing a town in the future. Trees in the region could be used for lumber and there might be useful minerals available for mining operations.

Taking on the base didn't look like it would be too easy either, O'Neal figured. The only advantage his team had was the fact the Angolans weren't expecting Kilembe to take the offensive. Security appeared to be minimal. There were no fences surrounding the installation; no surveillance cameras, no evidence of infrared eyes or motion detectors. O'Neal counted four armed sentries on foot patrol along the edge of the base and two guys posted at a small building near the motor pool.

According to information from the prisoners, the little building with the guards was the base armory. There appeared to be only one door and no windows. This suggested the information had been correct.

O'Neal passed his binoculars to the others and let them examine the site for themselves. If the mission was to succeed, it would require everyone to act in unison with precise timing and efficiency. They all had a pretty good idea of what to do before they reached the base. O'Neal cocked a thumb at Caine and pointed at the perimeter guard closest to the motor pool. Caine nodded. He understood that he and the three Pygmies were supposed to take out the two guards at the armory, as well as the outer sentry.

The Hard Corps commander gestured for Fanelli to take care of the closest sentry and gave the job of dispatching the guy at the opposite side of the compound to Wentworth. O'Neal would handle the last perimeter guard himself. The Kilemban soldiers would stay put for the moment and back up the others if the shit hit the fan.

Steve Caine and the three Bambute moved out first. They crawled silently through the tall grass, slithering into the shadows beyond the base near the motor pool. Crickets stopped chirping as the men approached. The guard nearby suddenly stopped pacing. He noticed the absence of the insects' song.

The three Bambute began chirping, imitating the crickets with remarkable accuracy. The guard stared at the shadows beyond, but failed to notice the prone figures hidden among the elephant grass. He turned and started to walk on, Kalashnikov rifle still slung over his shoulder.

He didn't see Steve Caine creep forward. The mercenary padded on cat feet and moved behind the unsuspecting sentry, the survival knife in his fist. Caine waited until he was certain the sentry was concealed from the view of the other guards before he made his move.

He struck swiftly, grabbing the man from behind. His free hand grasped the sentry's mouth to stifle any cry of alarm or pain as he plunged the knife into the man's left kidney. The guard thrashed about wildly in Caine's firm grasp. The merc quickly yanked the blade from his opponent's flesh and thrust the point into the hollow of the guy's throat to silence him forever. Caine lowered the guard to the ground and dragged the blade across the side of the man's neck, cutting the jugular and carotid with a single stroke.

He gestured for the Bambute warriors to come forward. One of them handed Caine's bow and quiver of arrows to the mercenary. Caine nodded and pointed at the armory. The Bambute promptly headed in that direction.

The Pygmies reached the rear of the building undetected. The elder warrior crept along one side of the armory toward the front of the building while the other two approached from the opposite side. Caine returned his survival knife to its sheath and prepared to notch an arrow to his bow in case the Pygmies needed backup.

The lone Bambute warrior crept forward in a kneeling stance, his spear elevated in front of him. He almost reached the corner of the building where the two guards were stationed. The Pygmy stopped and uttered a low grunting sound, a superb imitation of a pig foraging for food.

"*O que?*" a guard muttered as he stepped around the corner.

The Angolan soldier barely glimpsed the Pgymy before

it was over. The spear point caught the soldier under the chin. Sharp brass pierced the man's throat and split neck vertebrae. The Angolan's body convulsed briefly, impaled on the end of the Bambute's lance.

The other guard turned toward his partner, uncertain what the hell was wrong with his comrade. The other two Pygmies stepped forward, blowguns held to their lips. They exhaled hard and fired two darts into the side of the guard's neck. The man opened his mouth to scream, but poison had already frozen his muscles. The Pygmies grabbed him and yanked him off-balance. The man tried to struggle, but his neck was already swollen from the combination of hemlock and curare. The poison was already taking over his muscles and traveling through his blood to his brain.

Half-paralyzed and dying, the Angolan could offer little resistance as the Bambute dragged him around the side of the building. One of the Pygmies hastened the man's departure from this world with a knife to the heart. Caine was pleased with their performance in the field. He lowered his bow and crept to the armory to join his diminutive partners.

Although the two guards had been dispatched with very little noise, the shuffling of boots and sudden movement at the armory did not go undetected by the other sentries. However, the three remaining Hard Corps mercs were ready to deal with that problem.

James Wentworth III stared through the Bushnell scope mounted to his FAL. The cross-hairs were trained on the face of another sentry. Wentworth raised the rifle slightly, aware that the silencer attached to his FAL altered the accuracy of his weapon. The bill of the sentry's cap appeared in the center of the cross-hairs.

Wentworth squeezed the trigger. The noise-suppressor coughed with a loud pop—louder than a silencer in a movie, but still muffled enough to disguise the sound as a gunshot. He glimpsed the face of the sentry as the recoil of the FAL rode back into his shoulder. The man's nose vanished in a smear of crimson as a 7.62-mm bullet smashed facial bone on its way into the depths of his brain.

Joe Fanelli attacked another guard when the man turned to stare at the armory. The mercenary held two wooden handles in his fists with a foot-and-a-half of piano wire between them. He quickly swung the wire loop over the sentry's head, crossed the wire to form a noose and turned to place himself back-to-back with his opponent.

Fanelli bent forward to haul the guard onto his back and tightened the garrote in a "commando sling." The Angolan flopped about for a second or two, but the wire had already cut his carotid arteries, jugular, and windpipe. The corpse performed a few weak muscular twitches as the final traces of life faded away. Fanelli dumped the body to the ground and retrieved his rifle.

The last sentry had also been distracted by the actions at the armory and the mysterious report of Wentworth's muffled weapon. He turned his head from side to side, but his back remained turned toward William O'Neal. The Hard Corps commander moved behind the guard and raised his machete in a two-hand grip.

He swung the big jungle knife with destructive force and cleaved the heavy steel blade into the top of his opponent's skull. Bone split and sharp metal sunk deep into the man's brain. The Angolan's body barely twitched as O'Neal pulled the dead man to the ground. He placed a boot on the neck of the corpse and yanked the machete from the man's head.

So far, so good, O'Neal thought, but he realized the hardest part of the mission had yet to be completed.

Wentworth and Fanelli headed for the armory while the five Kilembans moved to the motor pool and hid behind vehicles for cover. Fanelli removed a set of lock picks from his field jacket and knelt by the door to the armory. He smiled as he inspected the padlock.

"Shit," Fanelli whispered as he inserted two picks into the lock. "I could do this sucker with a nail file."

"I don't care if you do it with your dick," O'Neal rasped as he joined the others at the armory. "Just get it open and hurry."

"Presto," Fanelli announced as he removed the padlock. "And open sesame."

He pulled the door open. The armory contained a veritable shitload of Soviet-made weapons. Racks of AK-47 rifles were chained to the floor. Dozens of PPS submachine guns and French MAT-49 subguns were also stored there. O'Neal quickly inspected the French weapons and noticed these had been converted to fire 7.62-mm ammo, the same caliber used in the Soviet weapons. The arms also included RPG-7 rocket launchers, some 81-mm mortars, and even two SA-7 Grail portable antiaircraft missile launchers.

"Jesus," Fanelli said softly. "Look at all this stuff. Lots of crates of ammo, and grenades, too. We done found the mother lode, Captain."

"We still gotta get it outa here," O'Neal muttered. "Joe, get the padlocks off those chains so we can move the rifle racks and crates."

"No sweat, man," Fanelli assured him.

"Sweat a little," O'Neal said softly. "We're inside an enemy camp, damn it. I wanna get outa here as soon as possible."

Fanelli got to work on the locks. O'Neal stepped outside to scan the base. Wentworth, Caine, and the three Bambute were watching the other buildings carefully. Nothing stirred outside the buildings, but lights were on in a number of windows.

O'Neal was rather glad to hear the faint buzz of music from a radio in one of the buildings. He was relieved that insects and frogs were chirping in the surrounding area. If it was too quiet it would probably mean someone else was listening.

However, O'Neal didn't kid himself that a hell of a lot couldn't still go wrong before they could return to Kilembe. He didn't know how long the guards had been on duty before they'd been killed. The base was certainly big enough to have a guardhouse with an OIC and NCOIC in charge of the guard shifts. One or both of them would be awake. Either might decide to check on the guys on duty and, sooner or later, they'd bring out fresh men to replace the guards.

They still had a lot to do and damn little time to get it done. How much time was just a matter of luck, and O'Neal never counted on being lucky. A good commander can't afford to be an optimist in combat.

"Got all the chains off," Fanelli declared as he emerged from the armory. "Now all you need is enough musclepower to haul this stuff outa here."

"Good work," Wentworth whispered to Fanelli. "Nice to see the skills you got breaking into bike racks is still useful."

"With all due respect, Lieutenant," Fanelli said, and raised a fist with the middle finger erect.

"Get to the motor pool," O'Neal rasped. He was in no mood for any bickering between Wentworth and Fanelli. He realized they were just easing the tension, but there was no time to fuck around, even for a second. "You know what to do."

"Gotcha," Fanelli assured him.

The merc from Jersey headed for the motor pool while the others stood guard watch on the activities within the base. Fanelli found the five Kilembans and informed them how things were going so far. Three of them spoke English and the other two spoke French, so communicating wasn't much of a problem for the moment.

"You pick out a set of wheels for us yet, Sergeant?" Fanelli asked Roger Tikiti, a Kilemban sergeant first class who had formerly been an auto mechanic in Zaire.

"Got two nice trucks," Tikiti replied with a smile. "Best in the lot, if you ask me, Major."

"Good," Fanelli said. "We'll use 'em both. Let me see the rigs and give it a second opinion."

Tikiti showed Fanelli the two ZIL-151 trucks he'd chosen

from the motor pool vehicles. Fanelli briefly checked the
tires, peeked under the hood, and checked the fuel tank.
The rigs seemed in good condition. Hard to say what might
be wrong with them, but they couldn't take the trucks out
for a spin to see how they handled. The Russian four-ton
workhorses seemed reliable and the fuel tanks to each rig
were full. That was all they could realistically hope for.

"Okay," Fanelli declared, nodding with approval. "Get
the tailgates down and start loading everything into these
suckers. Put the ammo in the first truck, toward the cab.
Less of a chance it'll get hit by a bullet that way. Okay?"

Tikiti and the others nodded.

"Fine," Fanelli said. "I got work to do on the rest of
the vehicles here. I'll join you guys after I get everything
done. Sergeant, you stay here and give me a hand."

Four Kilembans headed for the armory while Fanelli
slipped out of his backpack. He opened it and started to
remove packets of makeshift explosives. Fanelli and Tikiti
began planting the bombs under trucks and Land Rovers.
The Hard Corps demolitions expert attached blasting caps
to the explosives and hooked them to wires connected to
an insulated battery-operated generator. The device could
be turned on by a radio remote-control switch Fanelli carried
in his pocket.

"We've got one left, Major," Tikiti remarked.

"I'm gonna plant it under the fuel tanks of the gasoline
storage truck," Fanelli stated. "When that sucker blows,
we'd better be the fuck outa here or we'll wind up blown
to shit over this whole goddamn continent."

"That does not sound so good, Major," Tikiti said with
a frown.

"Let's just hope things go pretty much the way we
planned," Fanelli replied. "A job well done is fine, but
windin' up *well done* ain't so appealing."

The four Kilembans were carrying a rifle rack loaded with
ten Kalashnikovs. O'Neal followed, three RG-7 launchers

in his arms. They carried these to the motor pool, where Tikiti showed them which truck to load the weapons into. O'Neal checked with Fanelli to make certain all preparations in the motor pool had been completed. Then he followed the four soldiers back to the armory to collect more weapons.

Wentworth, Caine, and the Bambute warriors continued to watch the base for signs of activity by the enemy. The place seemed deserted except for music and an occasional silhouette in a window. O'Neal hoped their luck would hold out as he helped the four Kilembans with another load of weapons.

They continued the tiresome, tension-racked chore until all the rifles, launchers, and mortars had been packed into the two trucks. All that remained was to load on the crates of ammunition, rockets, grenades, and two boxes containing a couple dozen Makarov pistols. O'Neal and the soldiers hauled ten crates to the trucks, breathing hard from the exertion.

Suddenly, two uniformed figures emerged from one of the buildings. One man was an Angolan NCO and the other was a senior lieutenant. They headed straight for the armory and immediately saw the men carrying ammo crates.

"Ladrãos!" the sergeant cried, pointing at the departing figures.

The officer opened his mouth to yell for his men and clawed open the button-flap holster on his hip. Steve Caine pulled back the bowstring of his bamboo bow and released an arrow. The projectile shot across the parade field and struck the lieutenant in the chest. The steel tip pierced flesh and muscle and sank deep into the Angolan's heart. His shout was transformed into a loud groan. The officer managed to draw his pistol before the curare stopped his heart forever. His knees buckled and he crumpled to the ground.

Two Bambute blowguns hissed at the same instant. The Angolan NCO screamed as one dart pierced his left cheek and another poison projectile stuck in his jawbone. The NCO whirled and tried to run. The third Pygmy warrior nailed him between the shoulder blades with an arrow. The sergeant fell to the dust and crawled weakly a couple of feet.

One of the blowgun marksmen grinned as he loaded another dart into his weapon. He aimed at the fallen NCO and blew into the bamboo tube. The dart pinned the dead sergeant in a buttock. All three Pygmies giggled like school girls and pointed at the dart in the man's ass.

Their amusement over this silly joke ended abruptly as a burst of automatic fire erupted from the doorway of a building. The Pygmy with the Three Stooges sense of humor took three Kalashnikov rounds in the chest. The force pitched his small body several feet and sent it tumbling across the ground. The other two Bambute stared at their partner's still body lying in a growing scarlet pool.

Wentworth's FAL rifle coughed as he triggered the silencer-equipped weapon. He was in a better position to peer into the open doorway where the gunman had opened fire on the Pygmies. Wentworth triggered two shots, pumping both 7.62-mm slugs into the upper torso of the Angolan gunsel at the doorway. The AK-47 fell from the soldier's hands and he slumped across the threshold to topple down the steps outside.

Voices shouted throughout the base. A rifle barrel shattered glass from a windowpane. Caine promptly notched another arrow to his bowstring and launched it at the window. The arrow pierced the remaining glass in the pane and traveled into the building. The merc didn't care if the arrow hit human flesh as long as it discouraged anyone else from poking a gun barrel through the window. It succeeded quite nicely.

"Bug out!" O'Neal shouted, running for the motor pool with a crate of grenades in his hands. "Move, damn it!"

The others followed his example and retreated toward the trucks. A volley of bullets tore up chunks of dirt near the fleeing pair of surviving Bambute. The small size and surprising speed of the Pygmies made them difficult targets. They managed to reach the motor pool unscathed, still grinning despite their close brush with death.

A Kilemban soldier wasn't as lucky. A burst of 7.62-mm bullets cut a diagonal line of ragged holes across his back as he tried to shove a crate of ammo into the back of the second truck. Backbone broken, spinal cord severed, the trooper was dead before his body hit the ground.

O'Neal dropped the box of grenades, turned, and unslung his M-16 from his shoulder. He dropped to a kneeling stance and aimed the rifle at a trio of Angolan soldiers who'd charged from the guardhouse. They were green troops, unaccustomed to combat and poorly trained. The Angolan soldiers fired wildly at the motor pool as they ran and they failed to use surrounding objects for cover.

The battlefield punishes mistakes harshly. The Angolan troopers had made too many mistakes to live.

O'Neal fired a controlled three-round burst into his closest opponent. The soldier's arms swung overhead, tossing his AK-47 aside in the process. He lowered his hands to his bullet-smashed face, but he didn't live long enough to touch it.

Another soldier dived to the ground and tried to roll for cover behind a wood structure, which appeared to be a latrine. The guy had the right idea, but he'd taken action too late. O'Neal tracked the tumbling body through the sights of his M-16 and fired three 5.56-mm slugs into it. The man's body stopped rolling and came to rest for eternity.

The third soldier panicked and turned tail to retreat. He ran back for the guardhouse, dropping his PPS subgun as he fled in blind terror. The poor bastard didn't realize he was heading right into the path of other Angolan weapons, which were blasting away in the general direction of the Hard Corps and their allies. The guy was hit by bullets fired by his own comrades. His body jerked and twitched from the impact of the high-velocity rounds before he fell lifeless to the ground.

"Come on!" Fanelli shouted at the others. "Let's haul some ass. This place is worse than the South Bronx!"

Fanelli and Tikiti had hot-wired the two ZIL-151 trucks. The engines were roaring and ready to go. Two Kilembans climbed into the back of the first truck. O'Neal headed for the passenger side of the cab. A corpse was sprawled in his path. The Hard Corps commander jumped over it and glanced down at the dead man's face. The corpse was that of a member of the assault team. The Kilemban trooper had been shot through both lungs and the heart.

O'Neal yanked open the door and climbed into the cab. Fanelli sat behind the steering wheel. An unlit cigarette bobbed in the Jersey merc's teeth as he gripped the wheel so hard his knuckles seemed white as ivory.

"Pull out!" O'Neal instructed, swapping magazines to reload his M-16 assault rifle.

"I don't think the others have gotten into the next truck, Captain," Fanelli replied tensely.

"Pull out anyway," O'Neal insisted. "We can't help them by getting ourselves killed. Besides, this will draw the enemy's attention and give our guys a chance to use the distraction to their advantage."

Fanelli stomped on the gas and the big four-ton rig bolted forward. Bullets pelted the steel skin of the tractor-cab. One slug pierced the door near O'Neal and burned a bloodied crease across the merc leader's right thigh before it struck the dashboard and fell between O'Neal's feet. The Chicago-bred Hard Corps boss gasped, more from fear than pain.

Tikiti waited impatiently for the others to climb aboard the second truck. He sat behind the steering wheel, drumming his fingers along it and muttering every word of profanity he knew in English, French, and Swahili.

"Porco-cão!" a voice hissed.

Tikiti turned to the window of the passenger side of the cab. An Angolan captain stood on the running board with a Makarov pistol jammed through the open window, pointed at his face. He stared at the Angolan's angry features and slowly raised his hands from the steering wheel.

Incredibly, faced with death pointed right at him, Tikiti found himself wondering what the Angolan had called him. Roger didn't speak any Portuguese.

Suddenly, the Angolan's face exploded. Tikiti screamed with uncontrolled revulsion as the stump of the man's neck pumped twin streams of blood through the window to spatter the front seat.

James Wentworth pushed the headless corpse aside. He didn't even notice the unfired Makarov pistol in the dead man's fist. Wentworth flicked blood from the blade of his *katana* and returned the samurai sword to its scabbard before he opened the door and climbed in next to Tikiti.

"Merde alors!" Tikiti gasped, quickly recovering from the shock of seeing a man decapitated before his very eyes. "You cut off his head—"

"That's right," Wentworth replied calmly. "I believe I did. Get ready to move."

"I'm ready *now*," Tikiti assured him, nodding his head vigorously.

Wentworth peered back at the rear of the truck. A figure scrambled up into the back of the rig. The size of the passenger told Wentworth it was a Pygmy. The familiar tall, lean figure of Steve Caine appeared next. He saw Wentworth and gestured with his bow to signal the truck to go ahead.

Caine jumped up to the tailgate as the truck moved forward. He nearly lost his grip and had to discard his bow to hang on. Caine hauled himself over the top and landed inside as a bullet splintered a wooden slat above his head.

The mercenary peered out at the lunatic figure who was chasing after the truck. The man spat out a string of Spanish obscenities as he ran and tried to aim his pistol at the same time. The scene may have been comical if the guy hadn't been carrying a real gun loaded with real bullets.

Caine drew the bamboo tube from his belt and stuck it between the slats. As he placed his lips to the blowgun, Caine noticed the pursuer was a Cuban officer. He recognized the uniform from previous missions in Central America, but it was too dark to see what rank the guy was. Didn't really matter anyway.

He blew into the blowgun. Caine had previously inserted a dart in the weapon and his breath sent the projectile whistling from the bamboo muzzle. The Cuban suddenly stopped running and fell to the ground, hands clawing at the copper-wire dart that jutted from his left eyeball.

Both trucks raced from the base while Angolan troops fired at them and rushed to the motor pool to try to pursue them. Fanelli glanced in the side mirror and judged their distance from the base. He decided the second truck had also driven out of range of the destruction he was about to deliver.

Fanelli grabbed the radio-remote unit and pressed the switch. He didn't allow himself to think about the result of this action. He didn't consider the lives that would be snuffed out, the men who would be maimed or the terrible misery he would cause the Angolan soldiers. He simply pressed the switch.

The detonator triggered the blasting caps and set off the explosions. Trucks and Land Rovers within the motor pool burst apart like popcorn. Shards of metal and chunks of raw flesh were tossed in all directions.

The fuel tanker exploded. Flaming gasoline burst across the motor pool and splashed waves of fire into the nearby buildings. Half the compound was covered in fiery liquid. Fanelli was glad he couldn't hear the screams of the dying and badly burned men within the base. He masked his feelings with a wry grin as he turned to face O'Neal. ''Tilt!'' he said.

CHAPTER 17

"WHY WEREN'T THOSE bastards stopped at the border?"
Luis Perez demanded after listening to the report about the
attack on the Angolan military base.

"They crashed right through the roadblocks and drove
across the border into Kilembe," João Jangwa replied.
"After all, the border patrol didn't expect to be attacked by
two Russian trucks from *within* Angola. By the time the
patrol realized what was wrong, the enemy lobbed some
grenades at them and forced the guards to stay down while
they drove through. Simple, ruthless, and more than a little
crazy. But it worked."

"*Cristo!*" Perez spat. "Didn't anyone radio ahead and
tell the border guards to expect trouble?"

"Who do you think should have radioed that information,
Colonel?" Jangwa demanded. "Half the troops at the base
were either dead or seriously injured. Most of the rest received burns as well and those that were in relatively fit

condition were busy helping the injured.''

''They're lucky I don't have them all shot for failing to maintain order,'' the Cuban growled and slammed a fist on his desk.

''What would that accomplish?'' the Angolan asked, aware Perez was speaking in anger and didn't intend to execute any of the survivors. ''Haven't enough of our people died at the hands of the enemy without killing more of them ourselves?''

Perez didn't bother to reply. He had turned to face his wall map of Africa. The red pins of victories for his forces no longer outnumbered the black pins of the enemy. Now, for the first time in the conflict, a black pin was jammed in territory beyond the rebel nation of Kilembe. Angolan territory. Worse, the battle had been the biggest of the conflict, and the other side had won.

The Cuban shook with anger. The Republic of Kilembe seemed to get stronger every day and Perez was rapidly running out of time. Havana wanted the rebels crushed. Moscow wanted Kilembe to become a faded memory, like Biafra.

Luis Perez wasn't really very interested in what Havana or Moscow wanted, but he was concerned about his personal survival. If he succeeded in bringing Kilembe to its knees he would receive a real promotion to field-grade rank and his choice of assignments in the future. If he failed, he would lose his life.

He had everything to gain and everything to lose.

Marcel Baridi entered Perez's office. The Congolese captain seemed considerably more solemn than he had been in his first meeting. Jangwa wasn't surprised. Baridi had been in charge of the special assault teams disguised as Kilemban soldiers and Nilotic tribesmen. The plan to get the different elements of the Republic of Kilembe to fight among themselves had failed and Baridi had to accept part of the responsibility for that failure.

"The boats are ready, Comrade Colonel," Baridi announced in English. "The captain of each vessel is very experienced with the river. I assume you want to supervise the weapons and additional personnel."

"Supervise?" Perez smiled as he leaned his rump along the edge of his desk. "I'm going to do better than that. I'm personally taking command of the attack force."

"I'm not certain that is a good idea—" Baridi began.

"You'd better *hope* it's a good idea," Perez snapped. "Because you're coming with me. You speak French and some other languages that may be needed."

"But, Colonel—" Baridi started to protest, but he decided this was a waste of time.

"I want you with me too, Jangwa," the Cuban announced, switching back to Spanish as he addressed the Angolan officer. "There will also be Angolan troops on board the boats and I need a multilingual second-in-command to make certain everything goes smoothly."

"I'd rather get you a translator, Colonel," Jangwa replied dryly. "But I don't suppose you want someone else for this honor."

"If I'm going into a combat situation, you're going with me," Perez said with a cold smile. "I know you, Jangwa. You're a survivor. I don't like you much and I know you feel the same way about me, but as long as we need each other we can trust each other. So you're coming with me, Comrade."

Jangwa frowned. Colonel Perez had explained his plan to enter Kilembe by boat to launch a series of crippling attacks on the rebel nation. The original strategy had called for this to be done after softening up the new republic by dividing the population. However, Perez's plans changed dramatically after the failure of the terrorist tactics and the attack on the Angolan base.

Perez had previously intended to send in only one or two small boats with a handful of men disguised as fishermen.

The boats would travel up the Cuango River to the Kilemban border and agents would get off the vessels to set up new guerrilla raids against the enemy. Now, Perez had decided to increase the size of the invading force and carry out far more ambitious attacks on Kilembe.

Perhaps Perez was desperate because the time limit issued by Havana was running out fast. Perhaps he was upset because a Cuban officer had been killed during the attack on the base. Whatever the reason, Perez was determined to throw everything he could at the Kilemban Republic.

Jangwa suspected Perez may have had a personal reason as well. The Cuban's machismo had been offended by the boldness of the mysterious white strangers who'd been hired by the Kilemban government. They had done a better job of organizing and coordinating their troops. They had second-guessed Perez's strategies and seen through all his deceptions. Finally, they had even dared to cross the border into Angola, steal two truckloads of weapons, kill more than a hundred soldiers, and burn half the base to the ground. It was as if they were sneering at Perez, daring him to come out and face them like a man.

Whatever other flaws Perez might have, the Cuban was not a coward. He was a highly skilled fighting man, especially at hand-to-hand combat. The Cuban was a karate expert and a superb knife fighter. João Jangwa was a powerful man, physically stronger than Perez. He had carved up more than one opponent with a machete, but he hoped he'd never have to test his skill against Luis Perez. The Cuban was as quick as a black mamba and twice as deadly.

But Jangwa didn't like Perez's plan. The Cuban was too hungry for a victory over the men who'd humiliated him. Perez was rushing into the next phase of the military operation against the enemy. The tactic would either cripple the Republic of Kilembe and leave it virtually defeated, or Perez's forces would be destroyed.

"We have one week to select the best men for this mission," Perez announced, turning to stare at the wall map. The black pins seemed to stare back at him, like the tiny black eyes of a defiant opponent. "One week to make certain everything is ready. It's time that we showed this Kilemban scum what war truly is and prove to them that their mercenary friends from the West are mortal men. Flesh and blood who die like anyone else."

CHAPTER 18

EVERYTHING WAS COMING down fast and furious. The world media was printing more stories about the Republic of Kilembe. Photographs of weapons and equipment manufactured by Communist countries, which had been confiscated from terrorists, supported General Zabibu's claim that his country was under siege by Angola and the Cubans. This indirectly involved the Congo, and even the Soviet Union.

Accusations were flying in all directions. The governments of Zaire, Angola, and the People's Republic of the Congo still refused to recognize Kilembe as a separate country, but they denied any charges of aggression against the tiny self-proclaimed republic.

Although Zaire still refused to allow trade or diplomatic exchange with Kilembe, it was willing to lift restrictions at the border to allow individuals to travel from Kilembe to Zaire. Zaire nationals, however, were still not permitted to cross into Kilembe without special papers or authorization.

The United Nations decided to send a special observation corps to witness the elections in Kilembe. Peacekeeping troops would also be sent to guard the borders during the elections. Whether or not the UN would actually agree to voting on official recognition of Kilembe depended on how well the elections turned out. If people didn't show up at the polls, the Republic of Kilembe would be a joke.

The news was both a blessing and a problem for the Hard Corps. When the UN personnel arrived, the mercenaries' job would be over. Kilembe could have its elections, hope for recognition in the future, and eventually send the Hard Corps the rest of their payment after the mercs were back in America.

However, the enemy had increased activities against Kilembe with a vengeance. Terrorism had ceased for eight days following the Hard Corps' raid on the Angolan base, but this proved to be the calm before a violent and destructive storm. Apparently, the other side had decided to make a last-ditch effort to intimidate the Kilembans into abandoning their new democracy. If the citizens were afraid to go to the polls on election day, the republic would go down the drain whether or not the UN observers were on hand to see it fall.

The Hard Corps couldn't blame the civilians for being terrified. A dozen border patrol soldiers had been killed near the Cuango River. Many had been blown to bits, others shot, and a few had apparently been wounded by shrapnel or bullets and finished off by machetes and knives, or brutally stomped to death.

A couple of fishing villages along the Cuango had also been hit. Huts were blown to hell, civilians butchered by explosions and bullets. Men, women, and children had been shot, bayoneted, and hacked to death by machete blades. Joe Fanelli had examined one site personally and reported the grim news to the rest of the Hard Corps.

"There were goddamn craters left by the explosions," Fanelli explained. "Looked like shell fire or mortar rounds.

Damn accurate shooting, too. Bullet placement on the bodies looked pretty expert.''

"Professional job," William O'Neal mused. "Your trackers have any luck tracing footprints to figure out where the bastards came from?"

"From the river," Fanelli answered. "Seems like all the recent attacks have come from the river. Doesn't take a genius to figure out the enemy is cruisin' up the Cuango in one or more boats, blastin' the shit outa everything in sight.''

"Yeah," O'Neal agreed as he examined the map in his office. "But we've got surveillance set up along the river. Nobody's reported any boats except the usual fishing vessels.''

"The last attack was right where the Cuango River divides Kilemban and Zaïrois territory," Fanelli noticed. "You don't figure Zaire decided to join forces with Angola and the Congo, do ya?''

"Anything's possible," O'Neal allowed, lighting a cigarette. "We have to keep a watch on that possiblity. But we have problems enough. We can't spare enough people to watch the whole shoreline, for instance. Some decent sonar equipment would help, but we don't have anything like that.''

"Frustratin' as hell, Captain," Fanelli commented. "I don't think they've got a dozen airplanes in this whole country. Half of 'em don't fly and we can't get any decent aerial recon from those that do. No telephones and not enough field radios to go around. It's like technology came to a halt here some time around nineteen twenty-eight.''

"Yeah," O'Neal said with a sigh. "Kilembe doesn't have much of anything except courage and a desire for self-government. Pity that won't be enough.''

"You figure the country will fold regardless of what we do?" Fanelli asked.

"Wish I could believe otherwise," O'Neal answered. "Even if the United Nations meets to consider recognizing Kilembe as an independent nation, that doesn't mean it'll happen. Kilembe has too many enemies.''

"So what the fuck are we doin' here, Captain?'' Fanelli wanted to know. "Wasn't Vietnam enough no-win warfare for one lifetime?''

"We weren't hired to win a war, Joe,'' O'Neal told him. "We were hired to train their military, help them fight, and help 'em hang on until they had their elections. If we can keep them from being overthrown by force and help them to defend themselves in the future, that's all we can really hope to do. If we can hold off the enemy for a couple more days, our mission will be over. There's not a damn thing we can do for the Kilemban economy.''

"I'm afraid you're right,'' James Wentworth commented as he entered the office. "When their economy falls, so will the government. Jacob knows it, too, but he still thinks they can succeed somehow.''

"I hope he's right,'' O'Neal stated. "Where is General Zabibu anyway? We've got a very fucked-up situation on our hands right now and we can't locate the military commander of the Kilemban forces.''

"He's in the capital meeting with the president for preparations for the UN observers,'' Wentworth explained. "I already told him we're going to leave before the United Nations people show up. Press corps will be flooding in when that happens and we sure as hell don't need any publicity. Jacob agreed that one or two days won't make any difference. Actually, we can leave whenever we want now. We've upheld our contract.''

"I'd like to take care of the bastards who are using the Cuango River to launch the goddamn hit-and-run attacks before we go,'' O'Neal muttered.

"Seems we know everything about them except how they've managed to disappear after every attack,'' Wentworth said with a sigh. "Still no idea how they're doing it?''

"Camouflage,'' Steve Caine announced.

The tall bearded mercenary had quietly entered the office

in time to hear the latter part of the conversation. He smiled
at his partners as their expressions revealed that his statement
completely baffled them.

"What do you mean, 'camouflage,' Steve?" O'Neal
asked, slightly annoyed by Caine's coy attitude. "Don't
dick around, man. We don't have time for it."

"I just returned from a visit with Moshi's Bambute and
the Nilotic tribesmen led by Jiko. I told you about Jiko?"

"The guy who tried to turn you into a pincushion with
his spear," Fanelli remarked. "I suppose you and he are
good buddies now."

"Sure," Caine replied. "That duel was just a misunderstanding. Anyway, he told me his people have lived
along the Cuango for centuries. They've always done their
hunting and fishing along the river. They've also perfected
techniques for this. Since the birds, fish, smaller reptiles,
and such tend to be frightened away by humans and alien
forms such as boats, which are unnatural to the normal
environment—"

"This ain't the National Geographic Society," Fanelli
snorted.

"Let him talk, Joe," O'Neal declared. "Steve was in
the process of saying more words in his explanation than
he usually says in a month."

"I was just explaining how Jiko's people camouflage
their boats to hunt and fish along the river," Caine said,
suddenly self-conscious. "The Nilotic cover the boats with
natural foliage and use it to conceal themselves and the
vessels. Then they just wait for the prey to get close and
pounce."

"So you think the enemy have disguised their boats as
floating rice padies or whatever," Wentworth mused. "That
could explain everything."

"Okay," O'Neal declared. "We'll increase surveillance
along the river north of the last attack. Inform everybody
what to watch for. Big clusters of reeds that seem to be

unusually high above the water. Movement along low-hanging branches that extend across the river. You know more about this stuff that I do, Steve.''

''We headin' out to the river, too, Captain?'' Fanelli asked eagerly.

''Goddamn right,'' the Hard Corps commander replied with a nod. ''This could be the biggest battle of the entire conflict and our last chance to hit the sons of bitches before we leave Kilembe. We're not gonna miss out on the kill.''

CHAPTER 19

STEVE CAINE'S THEORY was right on target. A surveillance team stationed along the southeast bank of the Cuango River had radioed the Hard Corps when they spotted a suspicious "island." The four mercenaries reached the surveillance site about an hour after dusk. The spy unit consisted of only four men, including Lieutenant Felix Shanta, an English-speaking Kilemban who had originally been a Botswanan soldier before he joined the Kilemban movement.

"After you told us what to look for, finding the boats was children's playing, as you Americans say," Shanta remarked, scratching his left cheek, just below his eyepatch. The eyepatch seemed to enhance his roguish features. O'Neal wondered if the guy was really missing an eye or if the patch was just a bit of theatrics.

"You're sure you found the enemy vessels?" James Wentworth asked as the Hard Corps followed Shanta along a narrow footpath through the rain forest.

"Absolutely," Shanta assured him, pushing aside some

loose bushes to reveal his little surveillance outpost.

The outpost was a small clearing among a thick tangle of vines, ferns, and elephant grass. Shanta's three teammates sat on the ground, surrounded by the leafy green walls. They had few supplies, four Kalashnikov rifles, and two pairs of binoculars. The last items were used to peer through gaps in the foliage to observe the river beyond.

The site was ideal for the surveillance team to spy on the river without being seen by the enemy, but the cramped quarters and abundance of mosquitoes and other insects made the job less than fun. The Kilembans endured their assignment, though; they had known worse.

"The enemy have two boats, *oui*?" Shanta explained. One of his men gestured for him to look at something through a pair of the binoculars, but Shanta ignored him. "The boats are quite large. Big steam-engine boats. They disguised the boats to look like an island. Shrewd bastards."

"How do you know so many details about the boats?" O'Neal asked. "The camouflage they're using must be pretty shoddy."

"Not really," Shanta insisted. "You see, Colonel, we wouldn't have noticed the island was odd unless you'd radioed us to look for such things. First we noticed that the island was surrounded by young bamboo trees. Such trees growing along the shore is most extraordinary."

"*Où se trouvent les bateaux?*" Wentworth asked the soldier who'd failed to get Shanta's attention. "*Pouvez-vous m'indiquer, s'il vous plaît?*"

"*Oui, monsieur,*" the man replied, apparently relieved that someone had paid attention to him.

"Also," Shanta continued to explain, "we noticed the bushes at the center of the island appeared dried out. Even the trees looked like they were dying. How could this be on an island surrounded by water? So, look more careful and we see two separate cabins with big smoke pipes hidden behind the leaves. The trees, we learn, are really bushes tied to other bushes and stacked high to make them tall.

Cochons, oui? Yet, they are clever pigs . . ."

"That's a great story," Wentworth commented, peering through a gap in the foliage with his binoculars. "But you could have saved it for later. We have all the proof we need, gentlemen. The boats are headed this way."

"Sonofabitch," O'Neal rasped as he moved to the bushes. He jammed his binoculars into an opening and saw the situation for himself.

The boats resembled floating bamboo crops with piles of shrubbery in the center. Shanta had been correct when he identified the vessels as large steamboats, but no smoke rose from the stacks. O'Neal heard the growl of engines and realized the steamboats had been converted to motor power. He could appreciate the enemy commander's ingenuity. Generators would attract far less attention than smoke from the pipes.

Each vessel was about forty feet long and loaded with troops. O'Neal could only guess how many of the enemy were aboard. Forty or fifty, he reckoned, judging by the number abovedeck. The number of opponents wasn't as important as what they were armed with. O'Neal saw a couple of big problems mounted on the deck of the closest boat. The bamboo shields concealed portions of the long metal tubes mounted on tripod stalks. The damn things *could* have been fancy telescopes, but O'Neal didn't figure the guys on the boats had much interest in astronomy.

"Recognize those super-bloopers, Captain?" Fanelli inquired. The merc from Jersey had also been observing the boats through a pair of binoculars. "Type Fifty-two recoilless rifles or somethin' real similar to those ChiCom blasters the NVA used back in 'Nam. I think we found out how they blew the bejesus outa the border patrol and those fishing villages."

"Yeah," O'Neal agreed grimly, lowering his binoculars. "What's the range on the Type Fifty-two? Six thousand yards?"

"Closer to seven and a half thou," Fanelli replied.

"They're only about two thousand yards away and they're gettin' closer. Those suckers fire a seventy-five-mill explosive shell. They only got to fire one of those to fuck up our whole day."

"Let's see if we can't fuck theirs up instead." O'Neal turned to face Fanelli. "Figure you can handle that SA-Seven Grail?"

"I can handle it, Captain," Fanelli answered, but his expression was worried. "I'm just not sure it'll do what we want it to. The SA-Seven is an antiaircraft weapon. It fires an infrared seeker missile, which can hit a target six miles away."

"These targets are a lot closer," O'Neal reminded him.

"Yeah," Fanelli said with a nod. "But I'm not sure if we got heat-seekers or not. And even if we do, a heat-seeker is designed to go after the heat from a plane exhaust. Ain't designed to take out friggin' boats an' shit."

"Guess we'll find out," O'Neal declared. "Steve, you and Colonel Wentworth set up the mortar. You used those eighty-one-mill jobs when you were with the Katu back in 'Nam, so you take the gun. Jim, you'll be his spotter."

"Affirmative," Wentworth answered. Caine nodded his reply.

"Uh, Colonel?" Shanta began nervously. "You are going to radio for reinforcements. Aren't you?"

"There isn't time," O'Neal replied as he took his M-16 from his shoulder. "We gotta stop those bastards before they get outa range."

"But, Colonel," Shanta said and looked around awkwardly, "there are only *eight* of us."

"Yeah," O'Neal agreed. "I can count, too. You have your men get their AK-Forty-sevens and head north about three hundred meters. Move closer to the shore, but stay concealed."

"Sir, I hope you don't want us to actually set foot on the strip of beach by the shore," Shanta said, genuinely frightened. "You realize there are crocodiles in this area?"

"Crocodiles?" O'Neal raised his eyebrows. "Great big lizard critters with powerful jaws and big teeth—those kinda crocodiles?"

"Oui," Shanta confirmed. "There are thousands of them around here. The shores and the water are quite hazardous."

"I certainly hope so," O'Neal said with a wolfish grin. "Mother Nature might just give us a hand tonight. Better get your men into position, Lieutenant. Fireworks will start in about two minutes."

Unhappily, Shanta called his men together and led them farther north. O'Neal checked on the progress of his teammates. Fanelli had prepared the SA-7 Grail while Wentworth and Caine completed loading the confiscated mortar and estimating the distance to the enemy boats in the river. O'Neal felt the familiar sensations of anticipation and fear, the eagerness of impending battle and the mysterious lure of possible death.

God, he thought. *Why do we keep doing this shit?* The rush of adrenaline and the excitement of combat answered his question. Life is never sweeter or more thrilling than when it is placed in greatest jeopardy. No drug can compare with this sensation. No risk of losing money or property can equal the ultimate gamble of literally putting one's life on the line. No challenge is more compelling than matching one's skill, strength, and cunning against a formidable opponent in a life-or-death confrontation.

O'Neal understood why they did it. He knew why they'd keep doing it until they eventually gave up their lives in combat. O'Neal and his men all realized this was their fate.

And they knew that the jungle battlefield that night might indeed be their last.

"Ready to rock 'n' roll?" Fanelli asked Caine as he propped the SA-7 across his shoulder.

"Just waiting for the green light," Steve Caine answered as he knelt by the stubby, pipelike mortar.

"These aren't exactly ideal conditions for launching mortars,'' Wentworth complained, tracking the progress of the boats with his binoculars. "If a round gets slowed down passing through the tree branches overhead, it'll go off target for sure.''

"Nothing is perfect,'' O'Neal replied as he moved next to Caine's position to help with the mortar rounds. "Just do the best you can . . . and you'd better do it right.''

"Wonderful,'' Wentworth muttered. "Okay, Steve. Target is at one o'clock. Fire!''

Caine launched the first mortar round. The big 81-mm shell burst from the wide muzzle and sailed upward in a wide arc. It cleared the tops of the smaller trees and barely skimmed the smaller branches of the others. The projectile continued out over the water beyond.

It whistled as it descended. Enemy troops aboard the vessels ducked and covered their heads an instant before it hit. Water splashed as the projectile broke the surface less than a yard from the bow of the second boat.

"Missed!'' Wentworth declared. "Came down too far to the left. Make it three o'clock and on the double!''

"Want me to fire?'' Fanelli called out, holding the SA-7 missile launcher braced across his shoulder, eye locked on the sights.

"Not yet,'' O'Neal answered, shoving a fresh shell into Caine's mortar.

Steve Caine altered the motor to fire at the unseen target, which Wentworth claimed would be at "three o'clock.'' He didn't question the officer's judgment. The Hard Corps members believed in one another. They had faith in the abilities and decisions of their partners in a combat situation.

Wentworth watched the boats through his binoculars. He saw enemy soldiers dressed in the uniforms of the Angolan and Congolese armies get up from the decks. A slender figure clad in a Cuban army uniform appeared briefly near the stern of the first boat. He appeared to be giving orders as he pointed to the shore.

Soldiers moved to the recoilless rifles mounted on the

decks of both vessels. They turned the big black muzzles of the powerful 75-mm weapons toward the Hard Corps' position. Wentworth felt this stomach knot as he held the binoculars to his face with one hand and gripped the hilt of his samurai sword with the other.

Fanelli also saw that the enemy was about to blow them away. The demolitions pro had seen a lot of men blasted into oblivion. He'd killed hundreds of men with explosives himself. Fanelli had always wondered what it was like to die in such a manner. Would the blast kill one instantly? Was it painless? Or would there be a fleeting microsecond of unbelievable agony as flesh and bones ripped apart and vital organs were crushed by the force of the explosion?

The worse fear wasn't death. Fanelli had seen men survive after both legs had been blown off by explosions. He'd seen bloodied eye sockets after the orbs had been ripped out by shrapnel. He'd heard the screams of wounded men castrated by sharp flying metal.

Fanelli was ready to open fire with the Grail launcher. The infrared seeker had locked in on the port side of the first vessel. A green light indicated the weapon was on target. All he had to do was press the launch button. *Jesus!* Fanelli thought tensely. *Give me the fuckin' order to dust these bastards before they do us first!*

Fanelli held his fire.

Caine launched the second mortar round. The shell cleared the trees and whistled its one-note song of destruction as it sailed toward the enemy boats. Perhaps the heart of every man on both sides of the conflict stopped for the moment before the mortar shell landed.

The big 81-mm round of heavy explosives in metal casing exploded like a thunderclap. The cabin section of the second boat burst into pulp, sending a ball of fire into the air. Bodies were hurled over the handrails by the force of the explosion. Other soldiers, panicking, chose to jump over the side rather than remain aboard.

"Do it, Joe!" O'Neal shouted as he shoved another torpedo-shaped mortar shell into the mouth of Caine's weapon. "Fire!"

Fanelli immediately responded. He triggered the Grail launcher and saw a long comet-tail extend from the hurtling antiaircraft missile as it jetted across the river. The powerful AA rocket smashed into the port side of the first boat and the warhead exploded without mercy.

The blast literally broke the boat in two. Men were thrown into the river like rag dolls as the shattered vessel burst into flames. O'Neal patted Caine on the head and the stoic merc fired the mortar once more. Another hit. The vessel burst apart, spewing wreckage and human debris across the river.

"Wow," Wentworth remarked. It was the first time any of his teammates had ever heard him use this expression. It was certainly uncharacterisic of his usual vocabulary.

"How bad are they hit?" O'Neal called out.

"There's some bodies splashin' around out there," Fanelli announced. "Those boats are history, man. Nothin' left but some burnin' wood."

"Some of 'em might make it to shore," O'Neal declared as he grabbed his M-16. "Let's make sure nobody gets away. Be careful and watch out for the crocodiles."

"Croc-a-*what*?" Fanelli demanded in a startled voice. "Nobody told me nothin' about no goddamn crocodiles!"

"Don't you like surprises?" Caine asked with a thin grin as he gathered up his rifle.

The explosions and burning debris had frightened away many crocodiles that had been nearby in the river. But enough remained to do the job O'Neal was hoping for.

Screams filled the night. Fervent pleas in Kongo and U-Mbundu cut across the jungle. Figures splashed wildly in the river. Human hands beat the water hopelessly as powerful jaws snapped shut on flesh and bone. More crocodiles at the shore sensed fresh meat in the water and slid into the river to join in the feeding frenzy. The screaming soon stopped, but the splash of great tails, the ripping of flesh, and the crunch of bone continued.

Only five survivors from the enemy boats managed to
reach shore. One waded from the water at the north bank.
Shanta and his nervous followers opened fire on the poor
bastard and tore him apart with a dozen Kalashnikov rounds.
Two others staggered from the river, unarmed and ex-
hausted. Fanelli whistled to get their attention. The pair
gazed up at the M-16 rifle in Fanelli's hands and almost
gratefully surrendered.

Colonel Luis Perez half crawled along the muddy shore
toward the south bank, one fist pulling the collar of Marcel
Baridi's uniform tunic. The Congolese officer moaned
loudly and pawed at the bloodied mess at the end of his
right leg. A crocodile had bitten his foot off.

Perez dragged Baridi from the water and tried to draw
air into his lungs. The Cuban coughed and vomited in the
mud. He felt as if the gates of hell had opened up in the
middle of the river. He'd seen the first mortar round explode
and a second later he'd toppled over the side when the
antiaircraft missile split his vessel in two. Dead men had
already been floating in the water. João Jangwa had been
among the bodies. Perez had seen the Angolan's corpse
floating on its back with a section of an iron handrail driven
through the chest.

The Cuban swam for shore because there was no other
choice. The crocodiles had missed Perez, but one of the
beasts had grabbed Baridi's foot as he'd almost reached
shore. Under the circumstances, Baridi was glad to be alive.

Perez slowly raised his head and inhaled deeply. He wiped
water from his eyes and gazed up to find William O'Neal
standing in front of him.

"I'll be a sonofabitch," O'Neal remarked, pointing his
M-16 at Perez. "Didn't figure I'd capture a genuine Cuban
colonel."

"I'm . . . just . . . a . . . captain," Perez began as he
slowly rose to his feet. "Colonel rank . . . just . . . honorary."

"Small world," O'Neal said. "I'm an honorary colonel,

too. Unbuckle your gun belt, fella. Your English is pretty good, so don't pretend you don't understand.''

"Who are you?" Perez demanded as he fumbled with the buckle to his gun belt. "You CIA? Mercenary soldier?"

"I'm one of the guys who whipped your ass," O'Neal replied gruffly.

"Like you Americans say," Perez sighed, "can't win them all—''

He suddenly lashed out with the gun belt. It snared O'Neal's rifle barrel and jerked the M-16 muzzle away from Perez. The Hard Corps commander's trigger finger jerked and fired two useless rounds into the sand. Perez swung a karate kick and booted the rifle out of O'Neal's grasp.

The spring-loaded stiletto slid from under Perez's sleeve and into the Cuban's palm. The five-inch blade snapped into position and locked in place as he slashed a quick stroke at O'Neal's throat. The mercenary dodged the attack and raised his left arm to protect his face and throat. Sharp metal sliced cloth and cut skin. O'Neal ignored the burning pain and squared off to face his knife-wielding opponent.

Perez held the stiletto like an expert. He kept the knife low, feet in a solid stance, knees bent, and back arched. O'Neal stepped back, hands open and fingers arched like claws. The Cuban smiled, but he realized the merc carried a gun on his hip. He didn't intend to give O'Neal an opportunity to draw the pistol.

He decided to use a tactic that had never failed in the past. Perez faked a knife thrust, aware his opponent's attention would be concentrated on the stiletto. O'Neal's body jerked in response, a massive muscular flinch. Perez followed immediately with a high roundhouse kick aimed at O'Neal's skull. If he could bring down the American with a kick, finishing him off with the knife would be as easy as cutting into a steak.

However, O'Neal had been raised in a Chicago slum before he'd joined the Army and gone to Vietnam. Add on ten years as a professional mercenary, and William O'Neal had spent most of his thirty-eight years in street fights, gun battles, and outright wars. He knew better than to pay attention to only the blade in his opponent's hand. O'Neal saw Perez's leg move and ducked before the Cuban's boot swung for his head.

Perez's fancy karate kick missed. He nearly lost his balance and O'Neal delivered a kick of his own to Perez's left kidney. The Cuban groaned and pivoted, slashing with the stiletto. O'Neal's hand grabbed the wrist above the knife as he rammed a fist under Perez's rib cage.

The Hard Corps officer twisted Perez's wrist and seized the Cuban's damp hair to yank his head back. Perez grunted and reached back with his free hand to try to break O'Neal's grip. He also attempted to drive a bootheel into the American's nearest instep. O'Neal had expected something like that and shoved a knee into the back of Perez's thigh before the Cuban could deliver the blow.

Perez lost his balance and fell face-first to the mud. O'Neal held on and landed on top of his opponent. He straddled Perez's back, still holding on to the Cuban's wrist and hair. O'Neal pushed Perez's face deep into the mud. The officer from Havana struggled desperately and tried to break free of O'Neal's grasp. The knife blade danced wildly, but failed to find a target. Perez's free hand tried to pry off O'Neal's fingers from the back of his skull.

Suddenly, O'Neal released Perez's hair and grabbed the little finger of the Cuban's groping hand. He snapped the bone with a single hard jerk. Perez screamed. The stiletto dropped from his other hand. O'Neal stamped the heel of a palm into the base of his opponent's skull. The blow dazed Perez long enough for O'Neal to scoop up the stiletto.

O'Neal drove the blade into the back of Perez's head. Steel pierced the skull and sank quickly into the brain. Luis Perez's body twitched twice and lay still. O'Neal left him lying facedown in the mud. The Hard Corps leader staggered slightly as he walked to his fallen M-16 and retrieved his rifle.

James Wentworth III appeared along the shore. He glanced at O'Neal, the corpse of Luis Perez, and the moaning figure of Marcel Baridi. The Congolese officer appeared to have gone into shock, but Wentworth hoped he would survive; there were still many unanswered questions about the Congo's involvement.

"You okay, Bill?" Wentworth inquired, noticing blood dripping from O'Neal's left forearm.

"I'll live," O'Neal assured him. "Any other prisoners besides Mister One-Foot here?"

"Fanelli caught a couple of guys," Wentworth answered. "Nobody got away. We're sure of it. Guess this wraps up our business in Kilembe. Hope Jacob can keep up the struggle."

"Yeah," O'Neal agreed with a weary nod. "I bet Fanelli could use a good whorehouse now." He caught his breath. "Hell, I bet we *all* could."